SUSANE COLASANTI

So Much **Closer**

SCHOLASTIC

Scholastic Children's Books
An imprint of Scholastic Ltd
Euston House, 24 Eversholt Street
London, NW1 1DB, UK
Registered office: Westfield Road, Southam, Warwickshire, CV47 0RA
SCHOLASTIC and associated logos are trademarks and/
or registered trademarks of Scholastic Inc.

First published in the United States of America by Viking,
a member of Penguin Group (USA) Inc., 2011
First published in the UK by Scholastic Ltd, 2013

Text copyright © Susane Colasanti, 2011
The right of Susane Colasanti to be identified as the
author of this work has been asserted by her.

ISBN 978 1407 13083 5

Printed and bound by CPI Group (UK) Ltd, Croydon, CR0 4YY
Papers used by Scholastic Children's Books are made
from wood grown in sustainable forests.

1 3 5 7 9 10 8 6 4 2

www.scholastic.co.uk/zone

INVERCLYDE LIBRARIES

SUSANE COLASANTI is the author of *When It Happens*, *Take Me There*, *Waiting for You*, *Something Like Fate*, *Keep Holding On* and *All I Need* (Penguin US). She has a bachelor's degree from the University of Pennsylvania and a master's degree from New York University. Before becoming a full-time writer, Susane was a high-school science teacher. She lives in Greenwich Village, New York City.

www.susanecolasanti.com
Twitter @susanecolasanti

To my beloved city
of New York,
then, now and always

ONE

Today I'm telling Scott Abrams that I'm in love with him.

Sometimes I think that if he knew, he would admit he feels the same way. Other times I think he would laugh in my face so hard I would never get over it.

But.

It could be so easy. Just go up to him, tell him and see what happens. Put it all out there. Finally know how he feels about me.

It would probably be easier if he knew I existed.

The hope that Scott Abrams could like me back has kept me going for two years. It's like this energy I live on. The idea of being with him is almost more exciting than being with him for real. But of course I want to turn this fantasy into reality.

The thing is, he's never noticed me. Saying sorry because he accidentally bumped into me in the hall last year doesn't count. So telling him that I know we belong together is probably a crazy thing to do.

I guess I'm crazy then. Because I'm doing it anyway.

*

"You can't do that," April said.

Telling Scott was never some big plan or anything. I mean, yeah, I thought about it every day. I imagined how amazing it would be to let someone in. To trust someone completely. I just never thought I'd actually tell him. So it stayed a fantasy.

Then April and I were blowing up balloons for the junior picnic yesterday (she's more of a joiner; I thought it would be ironic) when it hit me. I would tell him at the junior picnic. It would probably be the last day we'd see each other until senior year. Plus, it would be the perfect time to start going out, with the whole summer ahead of us. The combination of being with Scott Abrams and two months of freedom would be the ultimate.

April didn't agree.

"Why not?" I said.

"Think, Brooke." April let the air out of a partially inflated red balloon. "What do you think he'd say if you told him?"

"I don't know. That's why I haven't told him yet."

"How many times have we gone over this?"

April had a point. She'd been hearing me obsess over Scott Abrams for two years. She was more than ready for a subject change.

"But you're assuming he doesn't like me just because he's never talked to me," I went. "We don't know that for sure."

"You're seriously going to do this?"

"Yes."

"After everything we've talked about?"

"Yes."

"Don't you care that—"

"No," I said. "I don't care if he tells the whole school. And I'll even tell Candice that I like him. I can't keep pretending we don't belong together."

"But how—"

"I just *know*."

I can't explain The Knowing. It's something I've had for as long as I can remember. There are certain things I just know, like when something crucial is about to change my life. It's only happened to me a few times, but when it happens it's undeniable. I'll get this intense feeling of clarity that forces everything else into the background. The Knowing is not supported by logic or factual information. But The Knowing is always right.

You'd think April would be less skeptical about The Knowing by now. We've been friends since eighth grade. She's been there. Well, she wasn't there for the hardest parts, but those things happened before we were friends.

Anyway. That's how I know Scott and I are supposed to be together. I've never been so sure about anything in my entire life.

There's always drama at the junior picnic.

For the past three years, major spectacles have occurred. Not *major* as in epic and intense. *Major* as in horrifying and wrong. Last year, Gina Valento went into labour reaching for a burger bun. Her water broke all over Mr Feinburg's nasty man-sandals. The year before, some kid broke this other boy's nose for keying his car. And the year before that, Ms Richter's trousers ripped open along the back seam. Like, a *lot*.

I really hope I'm not going to be part of the major junior picnic scandal everyone gossips about next year.

Scott Abrams is over with some other boys from the lacrosse team. He's not like them. I mean, Scott has straight, sandy-blond hair and very light-blue eyes and he's six feet tall, so he instantly fits in with any group of physically privileged boys. But I've been watching Scott long enough to know who he really is. He listens closely when people talk to him. He radiates confidence in a way that makes you want to be his friend. And he's really smart.

If you saw my report card, you wouldn't think I'm smart at all. But if school actually interested me enough to care about getting decent grades, things might be different. Mom always says how smart I am. This is usually followed by a rant about how I should be doing better in school or how I'm lazy or how I'm throwing my life away by "not working to my full potential". So the part where she says I'm smart gets annihilated.

Mom wasn't always this harsh with me. Before Dad moved out, she was much easier to get along with. Everything changed when he left us. It's like he was the glue holding us together. He moved out when I was eleven. It's been six long years of a strained relationship with my mom, which I don't think we'll ever be able to fix.

He ruined everything.

April pokes me.

Was I staring again? I was probably staring again.

Note to self: stop staring at Scott Abrams.

"Are you still going to do it?" she asks.

"Yeah."

"Do what?" Candice says. "Here's your lemonade."

"Oh, thanks," I say, taking the cup from her. "Um—"

April flashes me a look. "Brooke was just saying how she's getting that bag she wants," she tells Candice.

"The one from Mandee?" Candice goes.

"The one and only," I confirm. "We belong together."

"Is it on sale?"

"No, but there are only two left and I know if I don't get it I'll be mad at myself." I've been watching this bag for a few weeks now, waiting for it to go on sale. It's black with silver trim. Those are my colours.

"Oh, there's Jill – let's go and ask her about next week," April says to Candice. I know what April's thinking. The threat of leaving me alone to make a fool of myself in front of Scott is less serious than the threat of me telling Candice that I like him. So April drags her away, glancing back at me with pleading eyes like, *Don't do it!*

Scott is still hanging out with the lacrosse team. I

don't know how I'm going to get him alone. When I suddenly decided to tell him yesterday, my decision didn't come with instructions.

Then Scott goes over to the drinks table.

Alone.

This is my chance. I'm almost too nervous to take it. The thing is, it might be the only chance I get all day, and if I don't take it I might not see him until next year. So I force myself to go over to him.

He's rummaging through a cooler.

"Seen any Mountain Dew?" he says.

I turn around to see who he's talking to.

We're the only ones here.

Scott Abrams is talking to me.

"Um." I scan the soda cans. "No. Sorry."

He grabs a ginger ale.

Whenever I'm near Scott, he has this extreme power over me. He doesn't even have to be within visual range for me to get all flushed. Just knowing he's in the same building reduces me to a jangle of nerves. Being this close to him makes every cell in my body twang with anticipation.

He's holding the cooler lid open. "Did you want one?"

"Oh! Yeah, right. Sorry."

Note to self: stop apologizing.

"This is pretty lame," Scott says. Which means he's talking to me some more.

"Totally." I'm the one who's lame. For some stupid

reason I will never figure out, I'm still staring into the cooler trying to decide which drink I want. Which is apparently impossible to do while the boy I'm in love with is watching me.

Focus. Should I just come right out and tell him? Or should I ask if he can talk later?

"You do origami, right?" Scott says.

Wait. How can he possibly know that? I've been folding paper for years. My origami fascination started in seventh grade when Mrs Cadwallader taught us how to make paper cups. I went on to master the penguin, the dinosaur and the elephant. I'm currently working on a family of octopi.

"Yeah." I select a ginger ale. Scott closes the cooler. "How do you know that?"

"I've noticed you," he says.

"You have?"

"Didn't you do those ornaments for Ms Litchfield last year?"

"Yeah."

"Those were awesome."

"Thanks."

I *cannot* believe he remembers that. And what did he mean by "*I've noticed you*"? I've noticed how ordinary you are? Or I've noticed you because I'm in love with you, too?

With all the possible things I could talk to Scott Abrams about and all the backup scenarios I'd planned in case an opportunity like this ever came up, I can't think of one single thing that would keep him interested in this conversation.

It's time to take a chance.

"Scott, I—"

"Yo, Abrams, pass me a Dew!" Chad yells.

"All out!" Scott yells back.

"Pass me a Sprite!"

Scott throws him one. Of course the throw is perfect. And of course Chad snatches the can out of the air like it's the easiest thing. These boys aren't standard jock types, but they have this sporty/preppy physical language I will never be fluent in. I don't suck at sports, though. I'm flexible and I can run pretty fast. I even went running with my dad a few times, and that was back when I was a lot younger. Some of my mom's friends describe me as "wiry". I'm just not team-sports material. You have to trust people to be part of a team.

"Yeah?" Scott goes.

"What?"

"You were saying. . . ?"

"Oh no, just. . ." What was I thinking? I can't tell him here. Someone could come over any second. But it's not like I can ask Scott if he wants to go for a walk or something. That would be weird. This is the first conversation we've ever had. If you could even call it that.

"Nothing," I conclude.

He looks at me. He says, "Too bad we never talked before."

"We always have next year."

"No we don't. Well, *you* do. I'm moving."

Stop.

Scott Abrams is moving?

Heart.

In.

Pieces.

"You're . . . *moving*?"

"To New York. I hate that I won't be here next year, but my dad's job relocated him."

"When?"

"About three months ago they told him—"

"No, when are you moving?"

"Next week."

A bunch of kids race by, spraying Super Soakers at each other. My shirt is immediately drenched.

"Bummer," Scott says, looking at my shirt.

All I can say back is, "You have no idea."

TWO

Dad went above and beyond.

"I can't believe it." I gawk at the room. "This is unreal."

"So you like it?" Dad asks.

"Are you kidding? I *love* it." Dad was somehow able to get this room set up for me in a week. Apparently, it was his home office before. Now it's my new room.

In New York City.

The only thing I could think about all summer was Scott moving away. How he'd never know what he means to me. How he'd never realize that we belong together.

How I'd never find out if he feels the same way.

I keep replaying the things he said at the picnic. *I've noticed you. Too bad we never talked before.* A person doesn't say things like that if they're not at least a little bit interested in you. And the way he kept looking at me, like he was trying to tell me something. Something I'd want to hear.

I see the potential of us. I see what we could be together. If only I had one more chance.

When my dad left, he bought a two-bedroom apartment in Greenwich Village. I'd never been there, but I'd heard the neighbourhood was amazing. It sounded like the kind of place I belong. Even though the New York City skyline was close to my South Jersey town, it still felt so far away. Living in New York had been my dream for a really long time. I always hoped that I'd get to live there eventually, when my real life started. This was a chance for my real life to start way sooner.

It mattered to me so much that I called my dad.

That was a big deal. I hadn't talked to him since he left. Naturally, he was surprised to hear from me. He tried to keep me in his life when he left, but I didn't want any part of it. I didn't return his calls or visit him when he invited me. After a while, he gave up.

Which is why he couldn't believe I was calling.

"I'm so glad you called," Dad said. "I've missed you."

"Well . . . I know it was a long time ago, but you know how you told Mom I could stay with you?"

"Yep."

"Is the offer still good?"

"Any time."

Of course I didn't tell him about Scott. Just how I needed a change and how a better school would motivate me academically.

"I really want to transfer schools," I told him. "I've already looked into West Village Community online."

"It's one of the best schools in the city."

"I know."

"I'd love having you here," Dad said, all excited.

When forces beyond your control take over, they make you do stupid things. Or crazy things, like the way love was making me twist my whole life around. It felt amazing to even be thinking about moving. I also felt bad, though. I was lying about the whole school thing. Like I care where I go. But it was the only way to convince Dad that I had a valid reason for moving.

And it was the only way to convince Mom to let me go.

"What's this about?" Mom said, flopping down on the couch. I remembered when Dad used to flop on that same couch, exhausted from his long day at work and hectic commute home. It's still so weird to be in the same house with the same stuff, without Dad.

I had too much nervous energy to sit. I stayed near the coffee table, swaying a little.

I couldn't remember the last time I talked to Mom without feeling all tense. Ever since Dad left, it's like we can't even watch TV together without Tension cramming in between us like an unwanted guest who says they'll only be staying for a little while and then never leaves.

"If you don't feel like talking. . ." I said. Not that she ever felt like talking any more. But I should have known better than to try talking to her when she got home from work. She hates her job. Personally, I don't think there's any job she would like. Mom didn't work when Dad was here. She was a much happier person. Then he left and she turned all bitter and miserable.

"Now's fine," she said.

"Because we could talk later."

"Brooke." Mom rubbed her temple. "What is it?"

The grandfather clock in the corner ticked. The ticks sounded louder than usual.

"OK, there's this thing I want to do and I've already planned it out so you don't even have to do anything. All I need from you is permission."

"For what?"

There are two topics that infuriate Mom: school and my dad. I avoid these topics as much as possible. But if I wanted to make this happen, I had to bring up both of them.

"It's nothing bad. I um . . . I want to live with Dad for a while, is all. Just for senior year."

Mom barked out a laugh. "Why would you want to do that after everything he did to us?"

"Basically? I'm not challenged enough at school. And you're always saying how I need to apply myself more and how I'm not working to my full potential and everything. But I can't work harder unless I'm motivated. My school sucks. The school in Dad's neighbourhood is excellent."

"How do you know?"

"I researched it. There's a lot of money in that area. More money means better schools."

"Is that really why you want to live with him? To go to a better school?"

"Yes." I was totally lying again, but I didn't care. There's no way she'd let me move to the city and live with Dad just to follow some boy. "I have to show colleges I'm serious about improving my grades. Plus, I can write about my transfer for application essays."

Mom was sceptical.

"He said I could live with him if I wanted to—"

"I *know*. What he *said*."

"So . . . can I?"

"Absolutely not."

"Why not?"

"Is living with me so bad that you have to go running off to that manipulative bastard?"

Didn't Mom realize that anger was destroying her life? The Mom I used to know was so different. She used to plant flowers in the front yard every spring and play cards with the neighbours and volunteer at the senior centre. She would even surprise me after school sometimes with fresh-baked peanut butter cookies. Those were always my favourite afternoons, sitting in the kitchen doing my homework at the table while she started dinner. It felt really safe, like nothing would ever have to change.

I was so naive back then.

Over the last few years, Mom gradually stopped doing those things. Sometimes I don't even recognize her.

My leg banged against the coffee table, as if suddenly my brain couldn't control it any more. The remote control jumped. I wished it had a button for RESET CONVERSATION.

"He's not—"

"You only have one more year left. Then you can go anywhere for college."

"Well, I can't exactly get in *anywhere*, but—"

"Why are you doing this to me?"

So irritating. It's always about her.

"This isn't about you, Mom. It's about me."

"Well, you can forget it," she retaliated.

"I don't think so."

"Excuse me?"

"I'm not trying to be confrontational. You always think that, but I don't want to fight with you. I just want to go to a better school."

"It sounds like you've already made up your mind," she said. "It's not like I can force you to stay. So if that's what you want, fine. Let him deal with raising his daughter for a change."

"I just want to do what's best for my future," I said quietly.

"I don't like this."

"You don't have to."

So now I'm here. Staying with my dad. Going to a new school that starts in two days. All so I can be closer to Scott Abrams.

"My interior designer did a fantastic job," Dad says. "I can't believe this was my home office."

"She worked really quickly."

"That's what you get when you pay for the best."

I nod as if I can relate.

"My file cabinet used to be here." Dad gestures at a big dresser. It has that new-wood smell.

"I love it!"

"She thought you would. It's from Crate and Barrel."

"It's awesome. I totally needed more drawers."

Dad and I are off to a good start considering this is the first time I've seen him in six years. I think we're both trying to make things work. The way I see it, there's no reason for unnecessary drama after all this time. Which is probably why we're being extra polite to each other. And why my dad is giving me this incredible room.

He explains the other changes his interior designer made. I have a new desk and bookcase and night table, all in matching glossy white. The closet was redone so there's a section to hang clothes and another section that's all drawers and shelves and shoe cubbies. Light pours in from the two big, south-facing windows, a breeze puffing against the white cotton curtains. My bed is also from Crate and Barrel. It's way higher than my bed at home, with drawers underneath.

Obviously, I love my new room. I keep noticing more details. A round rug with bright stripes in the middle of the hardwood floor. Pillows on the window bench in colours that match the stripes. An apple-green beanbag chair. A shiny red stapler on the glossy white desk. A magnetic strip by the door with cool glitter magnets.

"I'm glad you like it," Dad says.

"Thanks for letting me stay."

"This is your home, too. It's great having you here, kiddo."

Kiddo punches me in the gut. That's what he used to call me. Back when he was a real dad.

Not that there's any point in getting angry about things that can't be undone.

I can't believe I'm actually here. After all that time wishing I could live here one day, this is suddenly real. Excitement fizzes through me, making me feel alive in a way I never have before.

It doesn't take long to unpack. I left a lot of my stuff back home. I mainly just brought clothes and books. And my wish box.

My wish box is the most secret thing about me. No one knows it exists. Not even April. I would feel like a huge dork explaining what it's all about. The box works like this: I put notes with my wishes in it. Then I hope. It's the only thing that keeps me sane, keeps me believing in the possibility of things that probably won't come true. But I have to hold on to that hope anyway. Hope is what keeps me going.

THREE

I moved here for a boy I don't know how to find.

At least we live in the same neighbourhood. That's what I heard from Chad when I ran into him at the Gas 'n' Sip right before I moved. So you'd think finding Scott wouldn't be that hard. Only, this is New York. There are like a zillion people on every block. We could live here our whole lives and never see each other.

My stomach is churning. I'm so afflicted that I can't even tell if I'm just nervous or also hungry. Before Dad left for work, he gave me money for the week. Then he told me where to get the best bagel and coffee – the most important survival tip, according to him. It was weird how he assumed I drink coffee instead of saying I wasn't allowed, like Mom. The stomach churn prevented me from eating before school. Now I wish I'd had something anyway.

I sneak another glance around the auditorium. This is the senior assembly, so if Scott goes to this school he has to be somewhere in here right now. Every time I look around, kids stare back at me. I force myself to quit looking. I don't want to get an instant reputation as a staring freak.

I took a risk by bringing my phone. If it gets confiscated, I can always say I didn't know the rules. I reach into my bag and check my messages. Still nothing from Candice.

In a lot of ways, it seems like every other first day of school. Everyone's wearing their best new clothes. Students are nervous. Teachers are handing out class rules that will soon be forgot. It's all new pencils and telling how your summer was and mourning the kind of freedom you won't have again until June. But in other ways, it's seriously different. The classrooms are relatively pristine. The teachers look and sound more professional. There's even a real discipline code. I was shocked to discover that there are actually consequences for not following the rules. My old school was huge, so you could totally get away with anything because no one even knew who you were. I get the feeling things don't work that way here.

By fifth period, I still haven't seen Scott anywhere. I'm beginning to think he doesn't go here. It's the only high school for kids who live in this school zone, but schools work differently here. You don't have to go to the school closest to where you live. Scott could go to some random school in Brooklyn for all I know.

Finding him is the only thing I care about. I didn't come here to make new friends. I already have April and Candice. Leaving them was really hard, but we'll talk all the time. And visiting will be easy – the train runs all day between here and there. Who needs more than two good friends? And what's the point of making new friends anyway? We're all going our separate ways at the end of the year. Eventually, everyone leaves. The closer you get to someone, the more it hurts after they're gone.

So yeah. I'm not exactly joining the pep squad.

Right before eighth period when I'm assuming that I'll never see Scott again for the rest of my life, I careen around a corner desperately searching for a room that apparently doesn't exist. The bell rings. I search my bag for my schedule to double-check the room number.

"Lost?" someone says.

"Sort of. Well, yeah, I can't find room two thirty-eight. Do you—"

I look up.

And there he is.

Scott Abrams.

"Hey," he goes. "I know you."

"Hilarious," I say. Because of course he knows me. He said we should have talked more. He said he loves my origami.

Except he's not smiling or anything.

Then Scott says, "How do I know you?"

World.

Shattering.

Apart.

"Um. I'm Brooke Greene. We went to—"

"Right! Sorry, I'm spaced. Trying to find two thirty-eight."

"Same here."

"Do you think it's a conspiracy?"

"All I know is, two thirty-eight should be somewhere between two thirty-six and two forty and it's not."

Note to self: do not burst into tears.

I would put this in the Of Course file if it weren't so tragic. My mental Of Course file is jammed full of stuff like this. As in, *Of course I moved all the way to New York for a boy who doesn't know I exist.*

But then there's The Knowing. I know that I belong with Scott. I know that I belong here.

"Should we ask in the main office?" I suggest.

"Good idea."

We get halfway down the hall before Scott goes, "Wait. Why are you here?"

"I go here."

"That's so weird!"

"I know."

"When did you move?"

"A few days ago."

"Why?"

There's no way I'm going to admit why. At least, not yet.

"Oh, because. . ."

Then again, if I just come right out and tell him he'll finally know. Isn't that why I came here? To make him understand that we belong together? The problem is, I might be the only one who can see the potential of us right now. If I scare him off, we might never be together.

I decide to go for the truth with a side of omission.

". . . I'm living with my dad now."

"Is that cool?"

"Yeah, it's awesome. I love it here."

"Tell me about it. Anywhere you can get a sandwich at three in the morning is my kind of town."

We get to the main office. The secretary is on the phone.

We wait.

When Scott leans against the counter, his arm brushes up against my arm.

Our arms are totally touching.

And he's not moving his arm away.

"Where's your dad's place?" Scott says.

"Perry Street."

"We're on West 11th."

"Aren't they near each other?"

Scott smiles. "Hey, neighbour."

When I answer the phone after school, April doesn't even wait for me to say hello. She goes, *"Oh my god you found Scott?!"*

"Yes! How'd you know?"

"Chad told me."

"Since when do you talk to Chad?"

"Since today. We both stayed after and he came up to me."

"But how does Chad know I found Scott?"

"Scott told him."

"What?!"

"I know!"

"When?"

"Scott called him right after school."

"What did he say?"

"Just that you have a class together. And he was really surprised to see you."

"He was?"

"Of course!"

"Like, surprised in a good way?"

"For sure."

Things are definitely working out. Scott and I live right next to each other. We go to the same school. We have a class together. We even get to sit together. By the time we found room 238, there were only two seats left in the front. My aversion to the front row was nothing compared to my desire to sit next to him.

Scott Abrams told his best friend about me.

It's a relief that April is excited about this. When I told her I was moving here, she wasn't exactly thrilled. April still thought telling Scott how I felt was a bad idea. She thought following him here was an even worse one. Even though she knew how I'd wanted to live in New York for a long time so it wouldn't be like I was just following some boy here, we both knew that I totally was. She didn't want me to get hurt any more than I'd already been. But by the end of summer, she was in my corner. She saw how miserable I was. She knew I had to do this.

I tell April every single detail about what happened with Scott today.

"I can't believe you got seats together in class," she says. "How perfect is that?"

"Seriously. Now I don't have to track him down like a creeper."

"So . . . when are you going to tell him?"

"I'm not sure. Maybe it's better to wait a while. I mean, I'll get to see him every day. Maybe I should give him some time to get used to me being here."

"That sounds good."

"It's really bad that he didn't recognize me, right?"

"Well, it's not the best. But it was his first day at a new school, too. You were both kind of out of it. I wouldn't worry – he told Chad about you and everything. I doubt he'd do that if he wasn't happy you're there."

That makes sense. We could dissect the situation for ever, but the only way to know what Scott thinks for sure is to ask him.

April and I compare our first days. I always knew my old school sucked, but now I have confirmation that it sucked way worse than I thought.

Then I say, "What's up with Candice? She hasn't responded to my last two texts and she's not calling me back."

"I don't know. Do you want me to ask?"

"Yeah. It's weird that we haven't talked for two days."

"I'll tell her to call you."

"Call me tomorrow."

"Of course. Good luck with Scott."

Luck isn't what I need. What I need is to know that I haven't disrupted my entire life for nothing.

FOUR

Scott could be in his room behind any one of these windows. He could be watching me right now.

I can't believe he lives one street over from me. That's one for the Of Course file. Of course we live closer to each other now than we did back home. The thing is, he could live anywhere on West 11th Street. It's several blocks long.

I've been walking up and down his street for over an hour. Just walking and wanting to find him. I love exploring my new neighbourhood like this. I'm so used to riding in cars. No one walked anywhere back home. But New Yorkers walk everywhere, and now I'm one of them. My legs are already complaining about the difference.

I stop. I want to be still for a minute and absorb the energy, feel how incredible it is to be in this place that's been calling to me for so long. It's like I already know it here so well, like these streets have somehow always been mine. Just being out on this warm night under the streetlights and neon, the excitement of finally being surrounded by everything I've imagined is exhilarating.

"Nice night," an old lady says, leaning out of her first-floor brownstone window. The window is wide open and she's watering the flowers in her window box.

"Yeah," I say. "I love your flowers." They're small ones in all different colours. They look happy.

"Thanks, I try. It's not always easy."

I nod without understanding what she means. Is it not always easy to keep flowers alive? Or not always easy to remember to water them? Or maybe it's a general statement about life. When is life ever easy? It's usually one problem after another. Like the problem of living with my dad.

It doesn't look like there's a problem from the outside. From the outside, it probably looks like a happy father-and-daughter reunion. The truth is that the past three days have been really stressful. Our conversations still have that polite tone. But underneath all that polite is a world of hurt. We both know it's lurking there. Except we're pretending it's not. All topics of conversation are kept on the safe side, like school (which I'm getting used to) and the city (Dad's planning for us to do some touristy things together) and college (I have no idea where I want to go). Dad hasn't asked me anything about Mom. I haven't asked him why he left us. What's the point of digging up a lot of stuff that's better off staying buried?

It feels like I've been searching for Scott's place for ever. He is nowhere. Eventually, I find this little cobblestone road that looks like it belongs in a different century. I slowly go down it, passing windows with warm lamps in them, families having dinner, people mesmerized by their computers. It's so different here. Back home, everyone closed their curtains at night. Here you can see right into almost every apartment. It's like New Yorkers are saying, *Look all you want. We know we rule.*

Suddenly, there's a highway, and then the Hudson River. I stood at my window on the other side of that river so many times, staring at the distant skyline like it held endless possibilities for a better life. Wishing to be on this side of things. And now I'm here. I've made it to the other side. And it's all because of Scott Abrams. He gave me a reason to leave my whole world behind.

There's a path by the river where a few people are walking their dogs or running or riding bikes. The air smells like fresh-cut grass. Everything looks new and clean. A sign says:

HUDSON RIVER PARK
OPEN UNTIL 1:00 A.M.

I'm exhausted from all the walking. I just want to sit somewhere and fold this piece of paper I found.

What I love most about origami is that there's always something new. You can never master everything there is to know, whether it's a harder design than the one you just did or a completely new one nobody's thought of yet. You can always do better than you did before.

You always get another chance.

I find this area with tall grasses and flowers and simple wooden benches. It's like some kind of Zen garden. I sit on a bench looking out at the river. Then I smooth out the wrinkles in my paper. Found paper is way more challenging than perfectly square precut origami paper. Found paper is real life. Real life isn't confined by exact dimensions. It extends beyond the boundaries. It comes with flaws. Things are never easy, especially when you expect them to be. Like when people disappoint you by turning out to be entirely different from who you thought they were.

People can be really corroded sometimes.

Recently, I mastered the origami giraffe. Now I'm trying a rhinoceros. It's hard to stay focused for more than a few minutes, though. This park is amazing. There's so much going on, even though it's getting late. All the people here and in boats on the river, tons of lit-up windows in the surrounding buildings, cars zooming by on the highway. No matter what time it is, there are always people getting stuff done in New York. Back in suburbia, everyone's probably inside watching TV right now, getting sleepy. They'll all go to bed around the same time and get up around the same time. But here, you can be free of those constraints. You can live this totally unique life that's all your own.

Just outside the Zen garden, there's a row of benches along the river. A girl is sitting on one of them, sketching something. It makes me really happy to be around people who are smart and artistic even if I don't know them. Just knowing that all of these creative types came to New York to follow their dreams is inspiring.

This girl looks like she's my age, so she probably grew up here. She's probably lived here her whole life. A pang of jealousy stabs at me. She's like this Sparkly City Girl who knows all these cool secrets about this place. Does she even know how lucky she is? Does she appreciate everything she has?

This is ridiculous. I'm jealous of a girl I don't even know.

I concentrate on my paper folds. But after a while, I look up again.

Under the glow of the streetlamp, I can see her profile. We both have the same shade of medium brown hair. Hers is really curly while mine's only wavy. And I think we both have brown eyes. If I could change one thing about myself, it would be my eye colour. My eyes are that boring shade of brown with nothing interesting going on. Sparkly City Girl probably has gold flecks in hers. She probably has a lot of things I don't have.

Whatever. I may never have all of the things I want, but one thing I do have is a fresh start. And it's up to me to decide what happens next.

FIVE

The class Scott and I have together is called Outside the Box. It sort of sounds like it might be fun. A class that's actually fun would be an entirely new experience for me. Supposedly, it's this combination of logic and creative thinking and something Mr Peterson calls "noodle cleaning". Someone asked what noodle cleaning was. Mr Peterson was like, "When it happens, you'll know." He seems pretty cool for a fifty-something teacher. He has this mellow vibe, like maybe he was a beatnik back in the day.

We didn't have any classes like this at my old school. I didn't even know you were allowed to have classes like this. If more interesting classes existed, then maybe the school system wouldn't be such a profound disappointment.

But this is still a class.

Which is part of school.

Which is evil.

The only reason I don't mind sitting in the front row is because I get to sit next to Scott Abrams. Normally, I avoid the front row. Sitting in the front makes you a target. Teachers call on you more. It's harder to avoid eye contact with them when you're exposed like that. And they assume that you're into participating if you choose to sit there, which in my case could not be further from the truth.

Sitting next to Scott means I get to watch how he writes. He presses down hard, scratching out quick little letters. When he turns to the next page in his notebook you can see the imprints of the words from the previous page. He's always fidgeting with his pen. He does this twirly thing with it where he quickly flips it over his hand. If I tried that, my pen would probably fly across the room and stab someone's eye out. Scott sits with one sneaker up against his chair rung. He's kind of too tall for his desk. He has this way of flipping pages in his book like he's trying to rip them out or something. He flips pages roughly, with purpose. I never sat close enough to notice that before. The closest I've ever got to Scott was last year when I sat two rows behind him in English.

This is so much better.

When the bell rings, everyone scrambles. This is our last class of the day. It would be pretty easy to talk to Scott now. Or I could just see if he talks to me first. I take my time putting my things away. Who knew this pencil was so fascinating?

"Hey," Scott goes.

"Hey."

"Can you believe this class?"

"I know."

"It would be practically illegal to have something like this back in Jersey."

"Seriously." *I moved here for you. We belong together.*

"So," he says, "see you Monday?"

"If not before."

"Right, in the nabe! Which reminds me — are you going to RiverFlicks?"

"What's that?"

"You don't know about RiverFlicks?"

"I just got here, remember?"

"Sorry." Scott flashes a smile that makes girls stare at him from across the room. "I've had the whole summer to investigate. It's this thing over at Hudson River Park—"

"I was just there last night!"

"Oh, cool. They do these outdoor movies all summer and tonight's the last one."

"What is it?"

"Excellent question." Scott considers this. "I forget, but it's a good one. I'm going."

"Really?"

"Yeah. You should come check it out."

"Maybe I will."

What does that mean, exactly? *You should come check it out.* Is he saying I should go just because I'd like it? Or was that supposed to be some low-key way of asking me out?

*

The movie screen is enormous. I can see the movie starting from all the way down the street. I didn't want to get here early. I didn't want to seem as desperate as I am.

That was a mistake.

Pier 54 is packed. There's a section of folding chairs set up right in front of the screen with space to sit on the grass behind them. Every single chair is taken. The grass is crammed with people. There's no way I could squeeze myself in. I keep searching for a free space along the edge of the crowd.

I don't see Scott anywhere. He should be here already. Maybe he's waiting for me. He might be saving me a seat.

This would be the perfect place to tell him. Outdoor movie. Moonlight on the river. The streetlights of our hometown glowing somewhere in the distance.

I carefully step over a leg, pressing up against the railing along the edge of the pier. I slink closer to the front, trying not to block anyone's view.

Then I see him. I had tons of practice memorizing the back of Scott's head from all that time staring at it in English last year, so I totally recognize him. He's sitting in the fourth row. It would be impossible to get all the way up there on this side of the pier, but there's a bit more space on the other side.

I cut across behind the chair section, ducking. Now I can see that Scott didn't save a seat for me. Maybe he tried. Once the movie starts, you probably have to give up the seat you're saving if the person you're saving it for isn't here yet. I hope he doesn't think I'm not coming.

Some folding chairs are leaning against each other on a cart. I don't know if you're allowed to take one. I should go for it. If I take a chair up to Scott's row, he could switch seats with the person at the end. We could still sit together.

I slide a chair off the cart. Before I realize what's happening, all the other chairs fall over. There's this huge clatter of metal chairs clanging against concrete.

Everyone turns away from the movie.

They all look at me.

Including Scott.

And the girl sitting next to him. Who is touching his shoulder.

He's with her. They're together.

He's here with another girl.

This totally goes in the Of Course file. Because of course Scott Abrams is here with another girl. Of course he wasn't asking me out.

Could I *be* a bigger reject?

After I make my way back behind the crowd, I start running. Three blocks away, I realize that I'm still holding the chair.

"Uuuhhh!" is all I can say when April picks up.

"Brooke?"

"Hi."

"You sound weird."

"Yeah, I usually sound weird after I've been mortified in front of the whole entire world."

"What happened?"

I tell her.

"Are you sure Scott was with her?" April says.

"Yes. She had her hand on his shoulder."

"That could have been—"

"He was *with* her."

"Blerg."

"I thought he wanted to go with me!"

"Who was she?"

"How should I know? I just got here."

"Have you seen her at school?"

"No."

"Maybe she doesn't go there."

"Maybe she's Scott's girlfriend."

"She could have just been a friend."

"I don't think so."

"How do you know?"

"I could tell." It wasn't as strong as The Knowing, but I immediately got this horrible sinking feeling in my stomach when I saw them together, like they've been going out all summer and I'm a complete fool for thinking I ever had a chance with him. "I could *not* have looked more ridiculous. Scott saw everything. Oh, and I stole a chair."

"What?"

"Nothing. I can't believe I was hoping this could work."

"You don't even know what he's thinking. He probably thinks it's funny."

"Do you think it's funny?"

"Um . . . it might be a little funny."

"This is so not funny."

"I know," April says.

I wish April was here. I'm not used to being by myself at night, and it's getting lonely. Dad had to work late. This morning I found money and a note on the kitchen counter, saying that I should order whatever I want for dinner. Dad was already gone by the time I woke up. He said he'd probably have to work late a few more nights, but that it's just temporary craziness. Some big client needs his attention or something. But how could he work late and not even come home for dinner when I just got here?

I shouldn't have moved. This was a ginormous mistake. I'm all alone. I don't know where anything is. I'm a total outsider at school. I don't know anyone. Scott doesn't count. He didn't even recognize me at first. I'm obviously thinking about him way more than he's thinking about me. And I really don't see that changing anytime soon. Because how do you convince a boy that you belong together when he's going out with someone else?

SIX

I've discovered the best coffeehouse ever. It's called Joe
the Art of Coffee and it's only a few blocks away. Mom
didn't let me drink coffee back home. But I would
drink it anyway when April and Candice and I hung
out at Bean There. What I now realize is that the stuff
at Bean There was merely masquerading as coffee. Joe
has shown me what real coffee tastes like. It is seriously
delicious. They even make these swirly designs on top
of the lattes that look like fancy leaf decorations.

The first time I came here, I felt intimidated. New
Yorkers are all so entrenched in their routines in this
way that makes you want to run out and get your own
routine. Everyone has these automatic motions, ways
that are totally ingrained into their daily lives. I feel like
a foreigner just watching them. So the first time I came
to Joe, it was awkward. I didn't know where to stand
after I ordered. I didn't know where the napkins were.
And were you supposed to leave your mug on the table
when you're done or put it in a bin somewhere?

Things are different now. I'm really comfortable
here. I could totally sit here all day reading or doing

origami. I even snagged the prized window table today. I'm attempting to dull the pain of seeing Scott with another girl by sipping my latte and reading a good book. It's about a woman who suspects that her husband is having an affair. I like books with plots about infidelity or divorce. I like being able to relate to the story I'm reading. It makes me feel less alone. All those books about shiny happy people are such a load. Real life is nothing like that. The best books make me feel hopeful when the characters' problems work out in the end realistically, not conveniently tied up with a big, red bow. Big, red bows are such a lie.

The little bell over the door chimes when a girl comes in. She squeals, "Leslie?!"

Something makes me look over to see who Leslie is.

It's her.

The girl from last night.

Scott's girl.

I really, really want to leave. But I just got here. I'm not about to give up my prized window table and bother the barista to pour my latte into a paper cup just because *she's* here. That would completely ruin the fancy leaf decoration.

I try to focus on my book.

A boy is watching me. He's at the other window table across the room. Every time I look over, he looks back down at his laptop. He seems a little older than me, like he might be in college. New York University is nearby. Maybe he goes there.

Eventually, the girl who yelled Leslie's name leaves. I've been keeping my head down while reading my book so Leslie won't notice me. She probably wouldn't even recognize me, though. It was dark out there. She only saw me for a few seconds before I ran off with my chair. I could have been anybody.

When Leslie gets up to leave, I slink down.

"Hey," she says to me.

Game over.

"Hey," I say back.

"Weren't you at RiverFlicks last night?"

"Huh?"

"*I Love You, Man.*"

"Excuse me?"

"The movie."

"Oh. Yeah, no. I mean, I stopped by to see what was playing, but then I had to go."

Leslie glares at me. A piece of hair is stuck to her gooey lip gloss.

"Scott said you guys went to the same school before you moved here," she informs me.

"He did?"

"Yeah. He did."

Sweet! This means he talked about me last night. He didn't just turn back around, watch the movie, and forget he ever saw me. Which is actually what I was hoping he'd do. But this is so much better. He *talked* about me. To the girl he was *with*.

Leslie is not as excited about this revelation.

She's all, "Just so you know? We're together."

"OK. . ."

"I go to Eames Academy so people at your school might not know Scott has a girlfriend yet? But he does."

If she's trying to impress with the whole Eames Academy thing, it's not working. I don't even know what that is. I'm just relieved she doesn't go to West Village Community with me and Scott.

"What does that have to do with me?" I ask.

Leslie smirks. "I met Scott right when he moved here. We've been together for two months."

Could she be any more insecure? She's a total train wreck.

Note to self: do not be intimidated by Leslie.

I sit all the way up in my chair.

"Congratulations," I say. "I'm sure you'll be very happy together."

She smirks some more. "Yeah, Scott said you were like that."

"Like what?"

"You know. Angry."

Scott said I was angry? I find that hard to believe. He doesn't even know me. How would he know how I am?

I throw my book in my bag and get up. A power couple armed with a fat newspaper and a laptop lunge at the table before I even step away from it.

As I pass Leslie on my way out I go, "You must have me confused with someone else."

Whatever. So I'm angry. You would be, too, if your dad left your mom for another woman.

It was worse than horrible.

I heard all the fights. I knew some of the reasons for them. Reasons I wish I could forget.

Things had been bad for a while. I can't remember when it started and I never knew why. All I know is that there was something wrong with my parents.

When Dad came home from his poker nights, Mom would drill him with questions. She'd ask him who was there and did he go out for a drink after and if so where did he go and who did he talk to? It sounded more like an interrogation than a conversation. Whenever they went out to a party or something together, there would usually be a fight when they got home. They'd hold out long enough to pay the babysitter. Then Mom would start in on Dad. I guess they assumed I was sleeping. But I was usually awake. And when they got to their room, I could hear everything.

A typical fight went like this:

Mom: So . . . Marie looked nice tonight.
Dad: Hmm.
Mom: Don't you think she looked nice?
Dad: I really didn't notice.
Mom: Her dress must have cost a fortune. Wasn't it fantastic?
Dad: It was all right.

Mom: I thought you said you didn't notice.
Dad: I'm going for a run.

Or this:

Mom: Who was Richard talking to?
Dad: Kelsey.
Mom: Who's she?
Dad: She's working with Dan on the Stevens account.
Mom: You know her?
Dad: We've talked.
Mom: At work?
Dad: Yes, Laura, we've talked at work. I work with her. We talk.
Mom: You never told me about her.
Dad: I'm telling you now.
Mom: Only because I asked.
Dad: [angry silence]
Mom: Does she work on your floor?
Dad: I'm going for a run.

Even though I was young, I was old enough to understand that Mom's jealousy issues drove Dad away. But after Dad moved out, Mom started telling me different reasons for why he left.

"Your father never knew what it took to be a decent parent," she ranted. "He was always looking for a way out, right from the start. I should have known things would end up this way."

Mom told me the kind of stuff you should never tell your kid. Even if it's true. I didn't believe her at first. But after hearing too many times how Dad left us because he'd rather have his freedom than be part of a family or how if he loved us more he'd still live here, I started thinking that maybe she was right. Maybe it wasn't entirely her fault.

Actually, I know it wasn't. Because before he left us for some woman he's not even with any more, there was that thing with my babysitter.

Justine was my friend. When she came over, it was never like she was just there to watch me. It was like she really wanted to be there. We told each other secrets. She'd tell me things about her life, things that mattered, like about college choices and boys she went out with and how it felt to be so close to the new life that was waiting for her after high school. I knew she would be leaving for college soon, but I hoped she'd go somewhere close so she could still come over.

Justine was like the older sister I'd always wanted.

This one time when I was ten, Justine was downstairs waiting for my parents to come home. I was in bed, but I wasn't sleeping. Then I heard my parents come home. I was always nervous when they got back from social events because I was never sure if they'd start fighting as soon as Justine left. I decided to sneak downstairs and see if Mom looked mad.

Except I didn't find Mom when I went downstairs. I found Dad.

And Justine.

Kissing.

I don't know if Mom knew about it. She never said anything to me. Of course I never said anything to her. She had enough pain in her life without me adding to it. But after that night, Justine never came back. She never even said goodbye.

People destroy your trust. Then they leave.

You can never completely know anyone, no matter how well you think you do. There will always be parts of their lives they leave out. There will always be some truth about them you don't ever get to know.

Or maybe one day you'll find out their truth. And you'll wish you never had.

SEVEN

Being inconspicuous was a lot easier at my old school. Here, there's nowhere to hide.

First off, classes are smaller. Even if I sit in the back row, I'm still way exposed. Teachers care more here. If you zone out, they call on you. If you don't do your homework, they make this huge production out of it. They even call home if you mess up enough times. Seriously, you can't get a break for one second. Like with calculus. Ms Jacobs is insane. She expects us to be ready to take notes right when class starts. She acts like we're supposed to pay attention to every little thing.

None of this is helpful when the boy you moved here for has a girlfriend.

I wish I could think about something else. Just focus on anything but the fact that Scott has a girlfriend who isn't me. This being calc, the only available distraction is a set of parametric equations.

I tackle them.

Avoiding classwork was simple at my old school. I know that everyone always says their school is the worst, but trust me, mine was the worst. You could totally get away with doing nothing, because the teachers never said anything. They would just give you a bad grade, which didn't faze most of the kids anyway. They hardly ever collected work. If they were going to, you could always just copy the answers from someone else. Lots of teachers didn't even read what we handed in. For most classes, your grade only depended on the quantity of work you did, not the quality. And people were actually surprised that I wasn't into school?

When I finish solving the last equation, I sneak a look at the girl next to me. She's still working on hers along with everyone else. Her name is Sadie, and she's wearing the same earrings as me – same silver hoops, same thin black stripes. Her look is actually kind of cool. She's got this whole Smart Sexy Girl thing going on, all shoulder-length copper hair with gold highlights, brown eyes that are more interesting than mine, and cat's-eye glasses. She's like two inches shorter than me and looks cute in everything she wears. She might want to rethink the headbands, though.

Sadie glances at my paper.

"How did you get that?" she whispers.

"What?"

"Number five. It's impossible."

"No it's not." I hand her my paper so she can see.

"You may ask your neighbour questions," Ms Jacobs reminds us, "but we're working individually." She looks right at me.

I am so not used to that. Teachers who make eye

contact freak me out. I used to be able to completely disappear in class whenever I wanted to. I could be invisible.

Not any more.

Sadie passes my paper back. She's like, "How did you *get* that?"

Playing their game is repulsive. Here we have one student helping another so she can solve some meaningless problem she'll never have to deal with in real life. I don't want to explain how I got it. I don't want to talk to Sadie at all. But it's better than thinking about Scott, which is what I'd be doing if I was just waiting for everyone else to finish. So I explain how I solved the problem.

"That's. . ." Sadie examines my paper again. "Where did you learn that thing you did in step three?"

"At my old school."

"Wow," she marvels. "You must have had an amazing maths teacher."

"Not really."

As I'm packing up my bag after class, Sadie goes, "Have you ever thought about peer tutoring? We're starting this week and I think you'd be great."

"Oh, that's OK."

"No, seriously. How fast did you finish those problems? People were still working on them like fifteen minutes later."

"I just wanted to get them over with."

"Yeah, but you got them all right. That's unbelievable."

It's official. Floating under the radar is definitely a thing of the past.

"We're meeting after school today," Sadie says. "Can you come?"

"No offense, but that's not my thing."

"What's not your thing? Helping people?"

OK, see, there's no need to get harsh. The girl doesn't even know me and she's being all insulting. I don't have time to explain myself to her. Of course I like helping people. I'm not a bad person. I just don't see the point of explaining stuff to a bunch of people who don't even want to be there. If I'm going to help people, I'd rather do it in a way that matters.

"Nice earrings, by the way," I tell her. Then I pick up my bag and head out, leaving Sadie behind.

"I have to work late tomorrow," Dad says. "I'll leave money so you can order in."

"OK," I go. But of course it's not OK. I shouldn't be ordering in by myself again. Dad should say that he can't work late any more because I'm here now.

Dad crunches into his egg roll. In the week that I've been here, we've had Chinese food, pizza and burgers from this place called Kool Bloo for dinner. It's fun to get takeaway all the time. It's like I'm on a trial separation from real food. We both know that Dad can't cook and cooking isn't something I enjoy, so homemade meals will soon become a distant memory.

"How was school?" he asks.

"OK."

"Are the kids nice?"

"They're OK." I haven't really noticed anyone besides Scott. Which is weird since I'm the new girl. I should be freaked out about fitting in and making new friends and who I'm going to sit with at lunch. But I'm not. Because none of that stuff matters. I'm only going to be here for a year. What do I care what anyone thinks? Plus, I'm sure April and Candice will visit soon. Not that Candice has returned any of my messages. She has to talk to me eventually, though. I can't figure out why she's not calling me back.

That's not entirely true. I have a bad feeling that she's mad because of Scott. She told me she wasn't and I believed her. But now I'm starting to think she wasn't being honest with me.

I squash the bad feeling down. There's no way I could deal with Candice being mad at me for liking Scott. That would mean I'm a bad friend and I just couldn't live with that. Maybe she's mad at me for ditching senior year. Or something else entirely. I just hope the bad feeling is wrong.

If I were going to be honest with Dad, I'd tell him that my day totally sucked. Scott didn't even talk to me in class. Usually, he says hey and we joke around a little. But today, nothing. It's like he totally shut down. Leslie obviously said something to him. Probably about how she ran into me at Joe and I was such a bitch, walking out on her when she wasn't done humiliating me. He probably thinks I'm some deranged stalker who likes to disrupt outdoor movies by clanging a bunch of chairs together. I can't believe Scott told her I'm angry. I didn't know it showed.

It's not like I want to be this angry. It just happened. If I knew how to not be angry any more, I would. The stupid thing about anger is how people hurt you and then you let them keep hurting you by being angry about how they originally hurt you. It's a vicious cycle.

Scott just met Leslie two months ago. How serious could it be? Maybe he's not technically her boyfriend. Maybe she thinks it's more serious than it is. Girls are often delusional that way.

Or maybe I'm the delusional one.

I just have to find a way to be in Scott's life more. It would be much easier for him to see that we belong together if he knew more about me. I should write a new note for my wish box later. Most of the notes in it are about Scott. I'm not sure where I'll be stashing my wish box yet. For now, it's pushed to the way back of a shelf in my closet.

Dad glances at the news, which is on in the living room. He can see the TV from his seat at the kitchen counter. It's like he's here without really being here.

I stab my chopsticks at some noodles.

He goes, "You have everything you need for school?"

"Yeah."

Then the questions stop. We just keep eating, with Dad watching the news and me stabbing at my noodles.

This is how we've been avoiding each other. When we talk, it's never about the things we really want to say. It's all just superficial how-was-your-day chitchat. The kind of words people say when the silence gets too loud.

The phone rings. Dad gets up to answer it. I assume he'll tell whoever it is that we're having dinner and hang up. But he doesn't do that. Instead, he takes the phone into the living room, gets on his laptop and stays there. I can't really hear what he's saying. Just some angry tapping of keys and tense tones. It's obvious that he's not coming back anytime soon.

I watch his food get cold.

EIGHT

A small piece of pink paper lands on my desk right before calc starts. It's folded once, with a smiley face in glittery purple ink.

I'm not surprised that it came from the direction of Sadie.

"What's this?" I ask her. Something tells me it's not just a regular note.

"Open it and see," Sadie says, all excited.

So I do. In loopy, round writing, is this:

Brooke—
We need your big brain! Please reconsider.
xo—Sadie

"It's a warm fuzzy," Sadie informs me.

"A what?"

"You've never heard of warm fuzzies?"

"No, but I'm sure you'll enlighten me."

"The purpose of a warm fuzzy is to spread the love. If someone needs cheering up or you just want to wish them a happy day, a warm fuzzy is perfect. And there are rules. Like how they have to be cute. They can't be written with a boring pen on some standard piece of paper."

Warm fuzzies sound sort of pretentious, with their rules and aspirations.

"And they count as random acts of kindness," she continues.

"Random acts of kindness?"

"Yeah. You know, doing things for other people for the purpose of helping them? Because you want to make their lives better?"

That sounds highly suspect to me. I don't believe that people do anything for purely selfless reasons. People's actions are motivated by their own desires. Every person who's disappointed me has been further proof that no one can be trusted.

I refold the warm fuzzy.

"Will you at least think about tutoring?" Sadie pleads.

Then the bell rings and, with her usual militant punctuality, Ms Jacobs starts class.

When Scott gets to the Box, he says hi. He even smiles at me. I could not be more relieved that the weirdness between us is over. Maybe he's one of those people who's automatically excited because it's Friday. I definitely like Fridays as much as the next person who doesn't want to be here, I just don't get whipped up in a frenzy about it.

Scott sits down next to me and pulls out a notebook. It's not his usual notebook for the Box, which is what everyone's calling this class. He's been using this ratty spiral with like ten pages left in it. This is a brand-new notebook. It has a black cover that says DUNDER MIFFLIN, INC.

"*Office* fan?" I ask. I know it's somehow related to the show because I just saw an ad for *The Office* on the side of a bus. The characters were standing under a big Dunder Mifflin sign.

Scott's like, "What?"

I point to his notebook.

"Oh, yeah. You?"

"Totally." Why am I being such a liar? I've only seen two episodes of *The Office*. And not even two whole episodes. Only a few random parts.

His face lights up. "That's so cool. I don't know anyone else who's into it."

It's amazing how quickly a day can improve. Even our classwork is fun. We're doing logic problems that feel more like a break than work that will actually be graded.

Someone calls out, "Can I get a drink?"

"The water fountain's broken," Mr Peterson says.

"Can I use the other one?"

"That would take too long. We have fifteen minutes left and I need you here for all of them."

Thirsty Boy glances at the sink in the corner, left over from when this room used to be the nurse's office. Apparently, he's not thirsty enough to bend down under the faucet.

"I can make you a cup," I say. I take a piece of paper

out of my notebook and fold it into an origami cup. "Here." I hold it out to Thirsty Boy.

"It works?"

"Yeah. Just don't take too long to drink."

He fills the cup at the sink. He gulps his water.

"Nice!" he says.

"That's awesome," a girl in the back declares. It's taking me for ever to memorize everyone's name. I don't know how teachers do it every year.

I grin at my notebook.

Mr Peterson is all over it. "What an excellent example of thinking outside the box!" he announces. "This was a terrific way to reach a creative solution. Many thanks to the always brilliant Brooke."

"Teacher's pet much?" Scott whispers.

"Not," I whisper back.

It's been an eventful day in the Box. Earlier, we found out what noodle cleaning was when we were working on a logic problem about astronomy. This one girl went, "I thought our solar system had, like, millions of stars," and Mr Peterson was all, "Our solar system contains only *one* star! Noodle cleaning in action!" He says there's all this erroneous information stuck in our brains (or, as he likes to call them, noodles) because we either learned things that were incorrect or we're remembering things the wrong way. He anticipates much more noodle cleaning this year.

"Listen up, gang," Mr Peterson says now. "I have a fun Friday treat for you. Logic pop quiz!"

Complaints rumble through the class.

Scott leans over to me. "Beer me strength," he groans.

I have no idea what he's talking about.

"Remember?" he says. "Jim and Andy?"

One of the few things I picked up during my extremely brief *Office* viewing was that the cute one is Jim. I nod and smile back.

Now we have a problem. I have a feeling Scott is going to keep quoting *Office* stuff at me. I can't pretend to know what he's talking about for ever. This could be a good thing, though. If we shared the same passion for something, it could be a way to be in Scott's life more, which I desperately need. Only, I don't like that show. The characters talk to the camera. I find that highly annoying.

So I'm not exactly thrilled, but I buy the first three seasons after school. It's weird what love can make you do. You do these crazy things before you can even recognize yourself. If it was anybody else, there's no way I'd start watching some show they like. Dad gave me a credit card for clothes and things, but he'll be checking the bills every month. I can justify my purchase because they're having a sale where if you buy three seasons you get a free shirt. Not that I want an *Office* tee, but Dad doesn't have to know that. The tee has a heart on it that says JAM in between the Jim guy and some girl. I don't know what "Jam" is supposed to mean. I guess I'm about to find out.

My plan was to discover where Scott lives over the

weekend. I thought about asking him where he lives exactly, but that would seem even more stalkerish. I tried to find out his address, but it wasn't listed. So I was going to keep searching his street until I found him. Except it rained for two days straight. I'm not a fan of walking around in the rain. I ended up staying in all weekend, having an *Office* marathon.

And now? I absolutely love *The Office*.

True, I only started watching it because of Scott. But oh my god, that show is *so* good. That talking-to-the-camera thing is actually really funny now that I get where it's coming from. And the whole Jim and Pam dynamic? Totally brill. I'm hooked.

On Monday, I wear my Jam tee to school. I nervously look around for Scott all day. I catch a glimpse of him down the hall before fifth period, turning a corner in the opposite direction. My heart flutters. I can't wait for him to see my shirt. It takes for ever for seventh period to end.

Scott's already at his desk when I get to class. I saunter over. He notices my shirt, smiling all big.

I go, "Is it just me, or does it smell like updog in here?"

"Yes!" Scott is so cute when he's excited. The only other time I've seen him like this was when his lacrosse team won state last year. "I love that one!"

We talk about our favourite episodes until class starts, tossing quotes back and forth. It's obvious I've totally won him over with my Jam tee. I like this Scott.

This Scott is interested in what I'm saying. It's easy to talk to him. Not that we're only going to talk about *The Office* from now on. It's just that I don't have to worry about what I'm going to say to him as much. We'll always have this. And once we have a few other things, we'll be so much closer.

The fun times continue. We get to work in pairs today, which means I can talk to Scott for the whole class. I'm on a natural high. We even keep talking after class and walk out together. Which is when I come back down to earth.

Leslie is waiting for Scott across the street.

He looks happy to see her.

And suddenly it's like I'm not even there.

It's sad how quickly a day can deteriorate.

"See you tomorrow," Scott says.

"OK."

Pretending to be waiting for someone, I watch Scott go over to Leslie. Her outfit is incredible. She's wearing an expensive-looking cropped jacket over a silk cami that I desperately want. Why does she have to be one of those girls who looks like she just stepped out of *Vogue*? I don't even want to know how much her jeans were.

Wait. Since when do I care about this stuff? I've never been insecure about my style. At my old school, kids complimented me on my clothes and accessories all the time. But here, things are a lot different. The urban vibe I thought I was rocking back home was nothing compared to what some of these kids wear every day. It's unreal. Except for a few unique pieces, I've been owned.

Suddenly, I feel like a big, fat dork, loitering on the sidewalk in my Jam tee. That doesn't even fit right. Why wouldn't Scott notice Leslie more? She stands out while I'm barely blending in.

Just when it seems like life is getting good, something always has to come along and ruin it.

NINE

Sadie wouldn't stop bothering me about becoming a peer tutor. It didn't matter that I wasn't interested. The girl was not hearing it.

So here I am. At my first peer-tutoring session. As a freaking peer tutor.

Yesterday in calculus, Ms Jacobs asked me to help someone with one of the problems. I didn't know that Sadie was watching me the whole time. Later, she pointed out how that girl was stuck on something that was beyond simple for me. Didn't I see how much I could help people?

I guess Sadie had a point. She was just so determined to get me here. Whatever. Maybe explaining stuff wouldn't be the worst thing if it makes someone's day a little easier. I can relate to feeling like you might not survive past second period.

Mr Peterson is the faculty advisor for peer tutoring. Before I could start, I had to take an aptitude test to see which subject I excel at. That subject will be the one I'll tutor. The aptitude test sort of reminded me of that IQ test we took in eighth grade.

I wonder if these results will be as major as those.

Even though the year just started, the tutoring centre is packed. I actually like it in here. There's room for all your stuff on the tables, and the chairs are really comfortable. The space is airy and bright, with big skylights. Finding a room at school where you can breathe is not easy. As an added bonus, there are cupcakes. Sadie brought them in from someplace called Crumbs. Apparently, she's a cupcake addict.

Mr Peterson comes back with my aptitude test.

"Huh," he says.

He just stands there, staring at the test. Not explaining the "*huh*".

I'm not about to ask. I don't want to appear too interested. Once teachers think you're interested in any part of the standardized testing/labelling/herding process, they assume they have you.

Mr Peterson sits down across from me. "Usually," he starts, "tutors specialize in one subject area. This test is very good at telling me what that subject is."

"Can't you just ask us what we want to tutor?"

"I do, but I also need to make sure you know your stuff. Sometimes teachers will recommend kids for certain areas, but since you're new I wanted to explore our options." He stares at the test again. "This is the first time I've seen results like yours. You seem to excel in . . . all subject areas. By a lot."

Is this the part where I'm supposed to be surprised? Because I've heard it all before. I still don't care.

"So can I just pick which subject I want to tutor?"

"To tell you the truth, I was hoping that you'd agree to be a general tutor. It would be great to have someone who could help out with everything. You'd be our first!"

I still haven't figured out Mr Peterson. His class is probably as cool as a class can be without violating any federal laws. But no matter how different his class is, he's still part of the system. The last thing I want to become is a cog in their machine. Just because I'm offering to tutor doesn't mean I have to be on their side, though. I can still make things work my way.

"OK," I go.

"Have you ever helped someone with a learning disability?"

"I've never helped anyone with school before."

"That's about to change."

After Mr Peterson goes over some guidelines with me he says, "We have some special-needs students who need help with all of their classes. I think we should pair you up with one of them. Does that sound good?"

"Sure."

"Wonderful! I'll send John over. He's a senior, too."

I watch Mr Peterson approach the boy who must be John. He's leaning against the wall with his earbuds in, playing air drums. He takes them out and talks to Mr Peterson for a minute.

John looks at me. Then he darts right over.

"Wow," he says. "You're my tutor?"

"Are you John?"

"Affirmative." He extends his hand like this is some kind of business meeting. "John Dalton, you're at my service."

"Excuse me?"

"Get it? 'Cause—"

"Uh-huh. Do you want to sit?"

John crashes on the plush chair across from me, turns his music off, and whips out an assortment of books and notebooks, all in one frenetic motion. His shirt says BIG GAY ICE CREAM TRUCK.

I get the impression that New York kids are way more accepting than kids back home. It's probably easier for gay kids to be out here. This city is so diverse. Kids are exposed to lots of different people and cultures, which probably makes them way more tolerant. No one would dare wear a shirt like John's at my old school. But no one in here is even looking at John.

"What's Big Gay Ice Cream Truck?" I ask.

"You've never been to Big Gay?" John is incredulous.

"Guess I missed that one."

"Dude, he's the *man*! This guy has all these crazy toppings, like bacon and pumpkin and pickles. He even makes his own toppings – so wild! He's usually at Union Square. Haven't you ever—"

"I just moved here."

"Oh. Well, I'll take you, we'll go, you'll love it."

"I'm Brooke, by the way."

"You rock, Brooke."

"Thanks."

"You're probably wondering why I'm here."

"Um—"

"I have dysgraphia. Ever heard of it?"

Yeah, I've heard of it. More accurately, I've read about it, which is why I still remember what it is. Lots of things I read stick in my brain, regardless of whether or not I want them there.

"Sort of."

"Basically, I have problems putting my thoughts into words on paper. Too bad we can't just hand in our brains instead of homework. Ha! Good one."

"So, maybe we could—"

"Work on my stuff, I know, I know. Sorry about the rambling. There's no excuse – it's just this thing I do. If you tell me to shut up, I won't be offended."

John's funny. Annoying, but funny. It's like we're already in on the joke together, on the same side of this academic war. But after a few minutes of working on his homework, his sense of humour vanishes.

"Why did I think this year would be any different?" he groans. "Of course it's just like all the others. Things don't get better just because you want them to."

"It's usually when you're wishing things would change the most that something gets in your way."

"Exactly! Why is that?"

"Who knows? I just put it in the Of Course file and slam the drawer."

"The what file?"

I explain.

"Righteous," John decides.

Not to be conceited (believe me, I'm nothing worth bragging about), but watching John struggle over such simple things is an eye-opener. I've helped people in calc, but those problems can be ridiculous. This is different. It's really hard for John to clarify his thoughts, even for easy questions. I've never seen handwriting like his before. There are random spacings between his words. His spelling needs a lot of work. And sometimes he mixes lowercase with capital letters for no reason. Mr Peterson said that John works with a specialist at school who focuses on his writing issues. He also has a private tutor who deals with dysgraphia. My job is to help him understand his homework and study for tests.

"You know in *Office Space* when they smash the fax machine?" John says.

"I've never seen *Office Space*." What is it with boys and office-themed entertainment?

"You've never seen *Office Space*?!" John says in this way where it's like, *Do any other movies even* exist?

"No."

"How is that possible?"

I shrug.

"OK, there's this scene – which you totally have to see immediately if not sooner – where the fax machine has been harassing everyone so these guys drag it out to a field and beat it up. They're all smashing it with a baseball bat and pounding on it and stomping it and pieces are flying everywhere. Dude. I can totally relate. All that anger and frustration is what I feel every day in this place."

It's official. John is awesome.

"Like with this quiz I just got back." He takes out a quiz with a red *32* at the top. I didn't even know they gave grades that low. I mean, I've got zeroes for not handing in work, but even when I do half of an assignment I somehow manage to get a passing grade on it. "I want to smash it. Except it wouldn't smash like a fax machine because it's just a piece of paper. An evil piece of paper. I'd want there to be pieces of broken quiz flying if I pounded it with a baseball bat."

"That would rule."

"I know, right? We'll have to settle for ripping it up with flair." John dramatically rips his quiz in half.

"Wait! We're supposed to go over that."

"Says who?"

"Mr Peterson."

"Rule number one of tutoring: throw out all previous rules. Seriously, if we stayed inside the lines on everything we're supposed to be doing, we wouldn't get anything done. Know what I mean?"

I do. Because John is speaking my language.

This tutoring thing might not be so bad.

Of course April knows all about my new *Office* connection with Scott and how I won him over with my Jam tee yesterday. And how Leslie was waiting for him after school. And how he looked really happy to see her.

"So what if he likes her?" April says. "Things can change."

"I wish something was actually happening with us."

"It is! You guys have more in common now. You have stuff to talk about."

April and I have been having these really long conversations every night since I moved here. I like to multitask when I'm on the phone. I'm currently working on an origami unicorn with the takeaway menu that was in my dinner delivery. Dad's working late. Again.

"If Scott talked as much as John, I'd be all set."

"Who's John?"

"I'm tutoring him." I tell April how Sadie was bothering me to join peer tutoring so I gave in. I tell her about John. I leave out the part about my aptitude test.

"Interesting," April says.

"What?"

"Nothing. It's just ... I never thought you'd do something like that. It's cool."

"Really?"

"Totally! It's obvious you want to help John. And it sounds like he really needs your help."

"I never would have started if it wasn't for Sadie."

April doesn't say anything.

"So ... what's going on with you?" I say.

"Guess who asked me out today."

"Oh my god, who?"

"Guess."

"Please tell me it wasn't Chad."

"No. Robby Miller."

"Robby *Miller*?"

"I know! How out-of-nowhere is that?" Robby Miller is this boy who was in book club with April last year. I really don't know anything about him. He largely goes unnoticed because he's so quiet. As far as I know, he's never even talked to April before.

"Do you even like Robby Miller?" I ask.

"I never really thought about him before. He's kind of cute. I guess."

"You should go for it. You're always saying how you want a boyfriend before we graduate. This could be your only chance."

"Thanks!"

"Not because of *you*. You're surrounded by a bunch of dorks. None of them are worthy."

"Except Robby Miller?"

"Possibly. Definitely worth investigating."

"I'll keep you posted."

"Hey, I still haven't heard from Candice. What's up with that?"

April stays quiet. In the background, I can hear people yelling and a car honking.

"Where are you?" I ask.

"Outside Bean There."

"Oh! I found this amazing coffeehouse in my neighbourhood. It's called Joe the Art of Coffee. Their coffee is on a whole other level. It's *so* much better than Bean There. We have to go when you come visit."

"I'll keep that in mind."

"Is Candice OK?"

"You can ask her yourself. She just got here."

Faintly, I hear Candice asking who's on the phone. April tells her it's me.

"Hello?" Candice says.

"Finally!" I yell. "I've been dying to talk to you! Didn't you get my messages?"

"And your texts and emails, yeah."

"Then why didn't you call me back?"

"Seriously?"

Candice sounds icy.

Hearing her voice like this makes the bad feeling come up again. But I'm still clinging to the hope that it's not because of Scott.

"What's wrong?" I say.

"What's *wrong*? How can you not know?"

"Um. . ."

"You knew I liked Scott. Not only did you try to get with him, you freaking *followed* him to New York!"

Crap. The bad feeling was right.

But see, I don't get it. How can Candice be this mad at me for liking Scott? When she liked him two years ago, she was super obvious about it. She didn't mean to be. It's just that her hormones took over. Everyone could tell she liked him. Whenever she saw him, she would turn bright red. She was always staring at him. The way she talked and acted changed whenever he was around. All the classic crush signs were there and everyone knew it.

The thing is, Scott didn't like Candice back. Someone eventually told him that she liked him. After that, he completely avoided her. He was clearly trying to let her down easy.

I couldn't just move to New York without telling Candice why. Especially since she'd heard that Scott was moving here. So I told her I started liking him right before she did, but that I'd been holding myself back because I knew she liked him, too. She didn't seem mad about it at all. She even helped me pack.

"But you liked him two years ago," I remind her.

"So what?" Candice snaps. "You knew I liked him. Who goes after a boy her friend likes?"

"I didn't know you were mad about this. Why didn't you say anything when I told you why I was moving?"

"Because I was trying to be a good friend. But then you left and it was real and now you're both. . . Why did you even move there? Did you really think Scott would suddenly notice you after all this time?"

Hearing Candice talk to me this way makes the guilt I was feeling instantly vanish. She obviously doesn't understand how important Scott is to me. And I seriously doubt I can make her understand.

"Talk about warped logic," she mumbles.

"I didn't think it would be a big deal," I explain. "You liked him a long time ago. He didn't like you back. End of story."

"Here's a flash: the world isn't black and white. There are shades of grey. You should try being more compassionate some time."

"And you should try supporting your friends. I gave up senior year with you guys. That's how much this means to me. Why can't you understand that?"

"Oh, I'm sorry. I tend to have a problem supporting my friends being backstabbing liars."

"When did I lie?"

"You didn't tell me you liked Scott. That's the same as lying."

"I told you before I moved."

"That doesn't count. The whole time you liked Scott, you never told me."

"Because I knew you liked him!"

"So how do you think it feels that you followed him to New York?"

"It doesn't . . . I'm sorry, but I can't protect your feelings for ever. I have to live my life."

"Go live it then," Candice says.

And then she's gone.

TEN

I like it here in the Zen garden. There's no sign or anything saying it's a Zen garden. That's just the impression it makes. I like the tall grasses, the minimalist wooden benches, the stepping-stones. I like how it manages to be secluded in the middle of everything while street life rushes by all around. Sitting here in the stillness, I think about everyone back home.

After Candice hung up on me last night, I felt so alone. April texted me after to say don't worry and that Candice will get over it. I'm not convinced. She's never been this angry before. But I really hope April is right. They're pretty much the only friends I have. I guess you could count Sadie as a new friend, but it's not the same. We don't have a shared history. I didn't realize how important that was until I left it all behind.

Everything is so different here. You cannot believe how many stores there are on one block. When I first got here I just stood on Bleecker Street, astounded by the abundance. You can pretty much get whatever you want within a few blocks of your place. It's unreal. And no one ever drives anywhere. New Yorkers take the subway or ride buses. They walk a lot. I've basically walked everywhere since I got here, which is a radical change. If you walked around back home, people would wonder what's wrong with your car. But here it's standard. People walk by you on the street remarkably fast, usually without even noticing you. Which is fine by me. I appreciate the anonymity. It's awesome that I could be anyone, that I don't have to be me when I'm sick of me.

But at the same time, it's kind of lonely. Dad's hardly ever home. I don't really know anyone at school. Things with Scott aren't the way I'd hoped. I miss my mom. We've talked a few times since I left, but it's not the same. Even though we weren't really getting along, having her home every day mattered. Seeing my friends every day mattered. I really miss April and Candice. I miss the things we used to do.

No more riding around in April's new car, singing over the music.

No more hanging out at Bean There after school, laughing about whatever.

No more scamming on boys down the shore all summer.

I take out my phone and call April.

"Hello?"

"Remember that guy down the shore who always put blue sunblock on his nose?"

"Who?"

"The guy with the blue nose. What was his name again?"

"I don't even know who you're talking about."

"Yes you do! He dropped his funnel cake on your towel."

"Oh." April's voice fades, like she's pulling away from the phone. "I remember now."

"Are you busy? I can call back later."

"No, I have way too much homework. Later is not an option."

Then there's this awkward silence. Here in the Zen garden, tall grasses rustle in the breeze. I wonder what's happening on April's side. I wish I could be in two places at once. Do I have to leave my old life behind completely just because I moved away?

"So how'd it go with Robby Miller?" I ask.

"It didn't. I'm still deciding what to say."

"But you want to go out with him, right?"

April sighs. I recognize that sigh. It's the one she does when she feels overwhelmed.

"I don't know," she says.

"Are you OK?"

"Yeah. I'm just . . . tired."

Something's not right. April and I can always talk, even when there's not much to actually talk about. I was hoping for one of our fun gossip sessions to pull me out of my mood. But it doesn't sound like April wants to talk about anything fun. Or even talk at all.

Candice has already moved on. Will April do the same?

"I should go," April says. "I'm never going to finish this homework. Call me tomorrow?"

"Do you want me to?"

"Of course! We're still us, it's ... sorry I'm being antisocial. It's just the exhaustion."

"I hear you. Talk to you tomorrow."

I'm not sure if I believe April about being tired. Whatever's going on with her, one thing is clear. The days of sharing my life with the only good friends I've ever known are over.

It's time to create a new life all on my own.

The girl who was out here sketching before is back. She's on the same bench as last time, looking up. I try to find what she's looking at. The moon is huge and bright.

Some people are running on the path between us. This is where Dad and I ran together the first Sunday I was here. He said how he needs to get back into running and I like to run, so we should run together every Sunday. That will be our thing. It's cool that it's only been two weeks and we already have a thing. We didn't get to run last Sunday because of the rain, though.

"Hey, Brooke!" a girl yells, running along the path. I recognize her from school, but I can't remember her name. I wave back.

The girl on the bench looks over. This jolt goes through me when we make eye contact. I've passed so many people on the street who zip by looking anywhere but at me. People racing by while walking their dogs or gripping their coffee cups or on their phones or speaking different languages with their friends. I don't know what everyone's in such a rush for. When someone does glance at me, they quickly look away if my eyes meet theirs. It's almost like there's this rule that you're not allowed to make eye contact with anyone for longer than two seconds.

Seeing someone and actually having them see me back makes an impact. Unlike the other New Yorkers I've encountered, this girl doesn't immediately look away. She smiles with friendly eyes. Then she goes back to sketching.

Maybe it's because I'm lonely. Or maybe there's something about her that I'm already connecting with on a subconscious level. Whatever the reason, I want to talk to her. I go over and sit on the bench next to hers.

"Hey," she says. "Do you go to Eames?"

"No."

"Oh. I thought I recognized you. I'm Rhiannon, but everyone calls me Ree."

"I'm Brooke."

"I heard. That's my sister's name."

Now that I'm closer, I can see the charcoal moon in progress on her sketch pad. Ree's moon has all these detailed craters that I can't even see when I look at the real moon.

"You're really good," I say.

"Thanks. It helps me unwind."

"Origami does the same for me."

I never talk this much to someone I don't know. I can feel some kind of magic happening. It's like the city energy makes anything possible.

"Do you live around here?" Ree asks.

"Yeah, over on Perry Street."

"Oh, sweet. I'm on West 11th."

She lives on Scott's street. That's one for the Of Course file. Maybe she's seen him around. She might even know where he lives. But how weird would that be, asking about some boy when we just met?

"I just moved here," I say.

"From where?"

"New Jersey." The skyline of Jersey City glitters in the night. I love its shimmery reflection on the water. I try to look in the exact direction of my town, somewhere behind that glowing line of light. But I can't figure out which way I'm from.

Ree still gives me a pang of jealousy, with her warm social skills and her Sparkly City Girl ways. She's had all these years to absorb the energy I'd been longing for. Being here is a given for her. I wonder if she takes it for granted. Or does she appreciate being here as much as I do?

"How's it going so far?" she asks.

"Good. I've wanted to live here for a long time. I'm living with my dad now."

"It must be nice having him around."

"I wouldn't know. He's never home." It happened again tonight. Dad didn't even call or leave a note this time. This working-late thing is obviously a permanent condition. He tried to be around more the first few days I was here, but then quickly retreated back into his normal routine. It makes me feel like I'm not even here, like he's not trying to make me a part of his life the way he said he wanted to.

"Same with mine," Ree says. "Is yours an investment banker?"

"How'd you know?"

"They're all like that."

I guess her life isn't as sparkly as I thought. Both of our dads ignore us. But I hope her dad didn't do the horrible things mine did.

When I get home, Dad hardly looks up from his laptop.

"Hey there, kiddo," he says like nothing's wrong. "How was school?"

"Fine."

"Good."

And that's it. He just goes back to his laptop. No apology for not bothering to tell me he was working late again.

It's really annoying how he can change my mood from mellow to snarly in two seconds.

I breeze past him on the way to the bathroom. I dump my clothes in the hamper and yank my robe on. I try to keep my anger under control while I take out my contacts. One of them almost gets ripped in half. Then I wash my face, remembering how peaceful everything was in the Zen garden, trying to think relaxing thoughts. Rage bubbles under the surface. Maybe I'll just go to bed early and escape.

But I can't. Because I ran out earlier without eating anything, so now I'm really hungry. I encounter a problem in the kitchen. I'm craving cereal, but there's no milk. What I'm craving even more is a home-cooked meal. Missing Mom's cooking is the last thing I expected to be doing, but there you go. Takeout was fun for a while. Now it's sort of sad.

My craving clamours for a bowl of Froot Loops. If I don't run out to the deli for milk, my craving will clamour even more. So I put on my glasses, throw my hair into a distressed ponytail, and pull on some old sweatpants with my vintage *Late Night with David Letterman* tee. I can't be bothered to put on any makeup.

Every night I search the neighbourhood, hoping to find Scott. I've walked up and down his street so many times I know those buildings better than I knew the ones on my old street. But I never just go out looking for Scott without getting ready. Before I leave, I usually try on at least five different outfits. I check myself in the mirror way too many times. The possibility of finding him is always so exciting. Besides sitting next to Scott in class, it's the best part of my day.

But tonight, all I want to do is grab some milk and come back home and eat cereal and go to bed. I don't think about what I'm wearing. I don't think about how I look.

So of course this is when I find Scott.

I'm just leaving the deli when it happens. He's kind of hard to miss. Since I smack right into him and all.

"Hey!" he goes.

I clutch my deli bag, saving the milk from falling at the last second. I do not look up. I cannot see Scott right now. More specifically, Scott cannot see me right now. I couldn't possibly look any worse.

"Um." I focus on the sidewalk. "Hey," I tell a passing car.

"On your way home?"

"Yeah, I was just . . . running out for something."

"That's cool."

"What about you?"

"I just got back from bowling practice. I know, it sounds lame. It's just there's no lacrosse team here, so I had to get creative."

"Makes you miss suburbia."

"Not exactly." Scott looks at my deli bag. "You hungry? I'm getting a sandwich – I found this phenomenal place."

"I didn't know sandwiches could be phenomenal."

"Are you kidding? Sandwiches rule."

Even though I must look like something that just crawled out of a gutter, Scott doesn't seem repulsed.

"So," he goes, "you in?"

"That depends. Would you mind if I went home real quick? I'm. . ." I gesture at my glasses and sweatpants. "Not exactly presentable."

"You look good to me," Scott says. He looks right at me when he says it.

This.

Is.

Happening.

We walk to my place. I try not to freak out that Scott Abrams is walking me home in this whole new city that I followed him to. I run upstairs, commencing the fastest reconstruction job ever. I'm not sure how much better I look five minutes later, but at least I'm presentable enough for a phenomenal sandwich.

On my way out, Dad glances in my general direction. "Going out again?" he asks.

"Just for a little while. I ran into a friend from school."

"Where are you guys going?"

"Down the street. For a sandwich."

Dad's already back on his laptop. "Have fun. Not too late, OK?"

"OK," I agree. Even though I don't know what "*too late*" is. We skipped the rules part of this arrangement when I moved in. Apparently, a lot of basic information gets left unsaid when there's so much else you're not saying.

"Ready?" Scott says when I come out.

"Starving."

He's right about the sandwich shop. My BLT extra B is seriously delicious. Scott's club sandwich is huge. It's so huge that I can't believe he can keep it from falling apart.

"That has to be the biggest sandwich ever," I say. "Is there anything *not* in it?"

"Crisps."

"Oh."

"And cereal."

Of course he said cereal.

"Did you hear about that guy who dislocated his jaw biting into a big sandwich?" I ask.

"Nuh-uh."

"Yeah, in Georgia. They're even naming the sandwich after him."

"I bet the sandwiches here are even bigger."

"This place is awesome."

"I know. How nice is it having more options than the fricking Gas 'n' Sip?"

So true. Back home, there was never anything to do. Everywhere closed early. Here the possibilities are endless. I like knowing I'm not the only one who's impressed that a sandwich place is open this late. The fact that I could see a movie at midnight — a quality indie movie — blows my mind. Or how crowded the streets are at two in the morning. Not that I've been out that late. I leave my windows open, so I can hear all the people outside. I love street noise. The sounds of traffic soothe me to sleep.

"So have you acclimated to West Village Community yet?" Scott asks facetiously.

"Hardly."

"Didn't you join that peer-tutoring thing?"

"How do you know?"

"Leslie told me. She's friends with a tutor who knows Sadie."

"Oh." I don't know which is more disturbing – that Leslie knows my personal business or that she told Scott about it. I want to ask if he's going out with Leslie, but it's obvious he is.

"She told me you guys ran into each other at some coffeehouse?"

OK. This is strange. Why is she telling him all this stuff about me?

"Yeah," I say. "Sort of."

"That's cool about tutoring. At least you have goals. I have no clue where my life is going."

"Neither do I."

"Really?"

"Why, does it seem like I do?"

Scott nods. "You come off like you have it all together."

"Yeah, right," I harrumph. "I wish I knew what I want to be. It's so annoying how everyone's always asking me that."

"Exactly! Like we're supposed to automatically know what we'll be doing for the rest of our lives. Guess I missed the memo on that one."

Scott finishes the first half of his sandwich. I stare at his arms. His sleeves are pushed up to right below his elbows. His arms are still tan from summer, all toned with sun-bleached blond hair. I don't know what it is, but I'm, like, hypnotized by certain parts of his body.

Note to self: stop staring at Scott's arms.

"I'm glad you're here," he says.

Does he mean here in the sandwich shop? Or here in New York?

"Me, too," I say, blushing. I never blush. That's how much power he has over me.

"Transferring to a new school for senior year sucks. Why couldn't my dad have waited until I was in college?"

"I thought you said he had to move for his job."

"Yeah, but I think he had a choice when to do it. He thought now would be better for everyone."

"Except you."

"Exactly."

Should I tell him? It's the first time we've ever been alone like this. I may not get another chance. Leslie could dig her claws in even deeper and then it would be hopeless. But what if he totally freaks out that I moved here for him? I mean, who does that? Telling him would be a huge risk. It feels like we've been getting closer. If I scare him off, I could ruin my chances for ever.

We talk into the night. I dreamed about being with Scott like this so many times, writing notes about him for my wish box, thinking up ways to get him to notice me. Now this night is here. It's real. And I have a feeling it's just the beginning.

ELEVEN

"Let's go to the High Line!" John says with way more excitement than I can take right now. The combination of attempting to navigate my way through the social structure of a new school, actually being required to get work done, and staying up too late has resulted in a catastrophic energy crash. After my sandwich shop interlude with Scott last night, so much adrenaline was zinging through my body that it took for ever to fall asleep. I barely had the strength to drag myself to tutoring today. I desperately wanted to go home and take a nap after school, but there's no way Sadie would have let me get away with that.

"It's tutoring time," I remind John. "As in time for you to be tutored. Did you get that trig test back?"

"Dude. It's precisely *because* it's tutoring time that we have to get out of here! What's the first rule of tutoring again?"

"Throw out all previous rules."

"Yes! Who says we have to stay in here all the time?"

"Mr Peterson."

"Mr Peterson also said we could relocate if we were so inclined."

"Really? He didn't tell me that."

"Go ask if you don't believe me." John leans back in his chair, putting in one earbud and firing up his music. His expression says, *I'll wait.*

I go find Mr Peterson. He confirms that we can have tutoring somewhere else as long as actual work is getting done. He's counting on me to make that happen.

"We can go," I report back to John.

"Like I said. Why would we even want to stay inside? Soon it'll be way too cold to go out and what kind of absurd waste of a perfectly good High Line would that be?"

"Just one question."

"Hit me."

"What's the High Line?"

John slams back against his chair so hard I think it's going to tip over. He drops his iPod, yanking the earbud out of his ear.

"*What's the High Line?*" he breathes, all incredulous.

"I'm new, remember?"

John puts his hand up like, *Give me a minute.* He struggles for composure.

"I'll tell you on the way," he says.

As we walk northwest (or "up and over," as John described), he tells me all about the High Line. It's a park, but it used to be an old branch of elevated train tracks that hadn't been used in a long time. The train tracks are still there, except now trees and flowers are growing all around them. They put in wooden lounge chairs that roll along the tracks and an area with bleachers where you can watch the street below through a glass wall. John even knows that the type of wood they used is called ipe, which was sustainably harvested from a managed forest.

"It sounds incredible," I say.

"Look up," John says.

There's an industrial metal structure elevated a few stories above Gansevoort Street. It's already impressive from over here. I'm also impressed by this triangular intersection we're crossing.

"Wait," I say. "I recognize this place." I look down Gansevoort Street at the cobblestones extending into the distance. The river glints against the horizon. We're right by a storefront that for some reason I think might have once been a flower shop. *Lewis King of Plants, 12½ Gansevoort Street.* Everything's coming back to me now. A scene from *Bed of Roses* was filmed here. It's this nineties movie where two typical New Yorkers (i.e. lonely people with baggage) find each other. Which I saw a long time ago, but of course I remember all sorts of details from it.

John goes, "How?"

"This was a flower shop in a movie. I can't believe it."

"Yeah. Lots of movies are filmed around here."

"That's so cool."

"I know! Dude, I love how you're stoked about this! Everyone else is so jaded. They're all been-there-done-that by the time they're seven. You tell them about the High Line and they're like, 'Who cares about some old train tracks?' It's tragic."

We climb the stairs up to the High Line. It's such an incredible space that it literally takes my breath away. It's like this whole other world up here, this secret level to the city you could just walk right by and never notice. As far as you can see, it's train tracks and all different flowers and trees and it's just . . . unreal.

John shows me all sorts of interesting things. I totally forget that I'm supposed to be tutoring him. He points out how all the energy-efficient lighting is at waist level or lower to cut down on light pollution. He explains that the vegetation is indigenous to the area, cultivated from locally grown plants. He shows me the red lights on top of some streetlights that used to be signals for firefighters back in the day.

"How do you know all this?" I ask.

"Research. Isn't it the best?"

I agree that it is the best.

What's also blowing my mind are all the upscale apartments right next to the High Line. Some windows even look directly out at us. That must be weird, having your private space being so public. When I first moved here, I couldn't believe how people left their curtains open at night. Now I totally get it. If I lived in one of these places, I wouldn't want anything blocking my view. Especially if I were on a high floor. Those views must be incredible.

It's seriously magical up here. The air is crisp. Tree leaves rustle in the breeze. My heart is happy.

We score an enormous bench made of gorgeous wood. John takes out his work. We manage to concentrate for approximately twenty-three seconds. Then John's like, "Check out that water tower!"

I've always had a thing for rooftops. I've just never really noticed water towers before. I guess New York has way more water towers than New Jersey, because suddenly they're everywhere.

"Which one?" I ask.

"That one right there."

"You mean the skinny one?"

"No, the fat one."

"The fat one's huge. He's hogging the whole roof."

"That's his prerogative. Look how commanding he is."

"I like the skinny one better. He has fringy edges. And a cool triangular top."

John squints at the skinny one. "Oh, yeah. That is cool. But not as cool as the fat one."

"Is too."

"You know I'm right. You're on my side."

"Am not."

"Are too."

"Not."

Silence from John. Then: "*So* are."

We really have to get to work. Except first we must take an inventory of all visible water towers. From this vantage point, you can see everything. I can see further into New Jersey than ever. But I still can't tell exactly where I'm from.

To prevent Mr Peterson from killing me, we stay late to get through everything we need to do. By the time we're ready to go, the sun is setting behind the river. It hasn't even occurred to me to watch sunsets since I moved here. The horizon is always blocked by buildings. But not up here. Up here is a whole other dimension.

"Aha!" John points to the fat water tower. "See why the fat one rules?"

He has a point. It's reflecting the sunset, glowing red and pink.

"It's amazing what you see when you look up," he says. "Always look up."

"Always look up. I love that." How many buildings have I passed without noticing their decorative details or rooftop gardens or penthouse apartments where you can totally see in? It's like I've only been focusing on half of what's here. I promise myself I'll look up more.

"Let's make an autumnal equinox resolution," John says.

"What's that?"

"This thing I made up just now."

"Nice."

"Yeah, so, what we do is . . . OK, here's how it goes. Tomorrow's the first day of fall. There's a different kind of energy when a new season starts, you know? So we're going to tap into some of that energy to sort of, like, renew ourselves."

I didn't realize boys could be like John. I mean, maybe in books and movies, but not in real life.

"We're making a resolution," he announces to the sunset. "Why should we have to wait for a new year to make resolutions? We can improve things any time we want. An autumnal equinox resolution – that's the best one! OK, what do you want to happen this fall?"

What I want to happen is obvious. Except it's not something I can share with John. If he ever found out I followed a boy here, he would think I was ridiculous. Not that I'm not ridiculous. I just don't want John to know it.

"Um . . . you go first."

John closes his eyes. He sits really still. I didn't know he was capable of sitting still.

"Your turn," he says.

"We're not saying them out loud?"

"We can next time, if you want."

It's a bit presumptuous for him to assume there will be a next time, but I guess it makes sense. I'm supposed to tutor John twice a week for the rest of the year.

I close my eyes and focus all of my energy on making Scott Abrams realize that we belong together. I resolve to take more chances with him.

Right when I open my eyes, the sun fades below the horizon.

"Which way are you walking?" I ask.

"About ten feet that way."

"You're staying?"

"Sort of. I live right there." John points to an apartment about five floors above us with huge windows overlooking everything.

"No way."

"Yup."

"I was just thinking how cool it would be to live in one of these places."

"I guarantee that it's infinitely cooler without your mother and little sister living with you."

"Where's your dad?"

"In Maine with his new wife."

"Ooh, sorry."

"Do you have any idea how cold Maine gets in the winter? And my sister Hailey is a pain to travel with. We have to divide holiday time between the parents now. Christmas is insane up there. You feel like a wild animal, all scavenging in the frozen tundra. No I mean, they feed us, it's just like your survival instincts kick in when it's that desolate."

Does anybody have a normal family any more? Apparently, it used to be extremely common for families to have two parents. They stayed together because that's what all the other parents did. Now there are so many options, so many different ways to be a family. So many ways to rip a family apart.

*

"So I hear you guys went to the High Line yesterday," Sadie says.

"It's amazing."

"I know." She zigzags on the sidewalk around an old lady who's shuffling along with a walker.

"Do you ever go anywhere for tutoring?"

"No, I like to stay inside. We get more done that way." Sadie randomly darts across the street. I run to catch up with her.

"Why did you cross? I thought Rite Aid was on that side."

"Oh, it is. I just always walk on this side of Charles Street."

"Why?"

"It's nicer."

I'm confused. Charles Street is one of the prettiest streets in the whole city. What does it matter which side you're on?

"I know it's weird," she admits. "I'm so used to my way of walking, I don't even realize what I'm doing any more. Sorry for being such a weirdo."

"That's OK." Walking with Sadie might not be the easiest thing, but it makes me feel less lonely. It still hurts that Candice is mad at me. Even April is acting strange. Yesterday was the first day since I moved that we didn't talk. At least things are improving around here. Sadie's not as annoying as I initially assumed. I think she's even someone I might want to be friends with. Which is why I agreed to walk home with her.

But first we have to go to Rite Aid. Sadie's out of tampons and I don't have any in my bag. I couldn't believe she didn't have any in her bag, either. Sadie's bag is massive. It's always loaded with supplies — lotion, mirror, sparkly lip gloss, gum, mints, nail files, assorted hair clips. You need it, she has it. Today is an anomaly.

In Rite Aid, I check out the magazine rack. John Krasinski is on one of the covers. I have to remember to tell Scott.

We get in line. Sadie takes out a small tube of Bliss Body Butter. I've noticed her use it a bunch of times in class.

"I like that body butter," I say. "It smells so good."

"My mom brings it home from work. She's a concierge at the W Hotel in Times Square — she gets tons of free samples. I'll bring you some."

"Thanks."

"Are you a Beatles fan?"

"Not really. Why?"

"There's this place in Central Park where people get together and play Beatles songs. It's called Strawberry Fields. Get it?"

"Um. . ."

"Like the song?"

"Oh." I probably should have known that. I do like some vintage music. Paul Simon rocks my world. His songs have such an amazing New York City feel to them. If there were a place in Central Park called "Train in the Distance" I would get it.

There are only two people ahead of us in line, but Sadie is all fidgety and flustered. I feel her pain. When I get my period, the last place I want to be is trapped in some line.

One of the cashiers shouts, "Next!" We're the ones who are next. But Sadie steps aside and lets the guy behind us go.

"Why didn't you go?" I ask.

Sadie is fascinated by a display of trail mix. "So how was the High Line?" she changes the subject. "Did you get any work done?"

"Eventually. I was pretty much blown away at first."

"Next!"

We're next again. Sadie smiles at the mother behind us who's pushing a stroller containing an unhappy baby. "You can go," Sadie tells her.

I'm like, "What's going on?"

Sadie turns away from the cashiers, studying the trail mix display again. Maybe she's embarrassed about buying tampons. I used to be like that.

"It's OK," I tell her. "I'll get them for you."

"Really? Oh my god, *thank* you." Sadie presses some money into my hand. Then she darts out of the store with her head down.

When I find her outside, she's leaning against the side of the store, all flushed. I hand her the bag and her change. "I used to hate buying tampons, too."

"That's not it."

"Then what's wrong?"

"Nothing. Can we just go?"

"Why—"

"I really don't feel like talking about it."

"OK."

We walk for half a block in silence.

Then Sadie's like, "Whatever, it's just . . . I was trying to time it so we'd get the other cashier."

"That's why you let those people go ahead?"

"Sort of. Yeah."

"I thought you were embarrassed about buying tampons."

"If I had to buy them from Carlos, I'd be mortified."

Of course that's why she was all jittery and flushed. She likes the cute cashier.

"He's cute," I say.

"He's beyond cute."

"If you didn't want him to see you, why didn't we just go to Walgreens or something?"

"He wasn't supposed to be there. He must have switched shifts with someone."

"You know his schedule?"

"No. I've just never seen him in the afternoons. Except on weekends."

"Have you ever talked to him?"

"Just the typical how-are-you-I'm-good stuff. But I swear he looks at me differently. As soon as he sees me, he gets all happy. I've watched him with other customers and he's never psyched to see them. I could just be imagining things, though. I probably am."

I'm sure Sadie's right about the way Carlos is with her. Why wouldn't he like her? She's totally cute and sweet. She's exactly the kind of girl he would like. Doesn't she know that?

"Whatever," she goes. "He probably has a girlfriend."

"You don't know that. Why don't you ask him out?"

"Oh yeah, right! Like he'd go out with me!"

"Why not? You're cute."

Sadie scoffs.

"You *are*. If you asked Carlos out, he'd be crazy excited."

"Then why doesn't he just ask me out?"

"You can't ask out customers. That's against the rules."

"So . . . what, I'm supposed to go up to him and ask him out?"

"Pretty much, yeah."

"I don't have that kind of confidence."

"Since when? You're totally confident."

"I lack boy confidence."

Do I have boy confidence? I think so. I've never been shy around them. Back home, people used to say that I came off as tough. Which is so weird because I don't feel tough at all. I feel broken. But now that I'm surrounded by possibility, it finally feels like I can put the pieces of me back together.

TWELVE

Scott is having a bad day.

He would get like this back home sometimes. I remember those days watching him from two rows back, how he'd be all slumped down in his chair. He was like a different person on his bad days. He'd completely shut down. I always wanted to ask him what was wrong and see if there was anything I could do. But I never found the courage.

And now we're friends. We sit together in class. I can talk to him whenever I want.

The second Scott got to class, I knew he was having another one of his bad days. I wanted to ask him what was wrong right away, but I didn't want to freak him out by knowing something was wrong just from looking at him. I have to say something, though. It's breaking my heart to see him like this. I consider taking a humorous approach. John would probably say, "Sounds like somebody's got a case of the Mondays!" which is this line from *Office Space*. Something tells me Scott wouldn't think it's as funny.

We walk out together after class.

"Are you OK?" I ask.

"No."

"Do you want to talk about it?"

"No."

Leslie is waiting for Scott across the street again. Since that psycho confrontation at Joe, she hasn't bothered me. Except for the way she watches Scott and me when we walk out together, like I have no right to be here.

"Well, if you change your mind, you know where to find me," I say. I also know where to find him. Because of course I searched for Scott all those nights and then we ended up going by his place after our sandwich-shop interlude. I love knowing exactly where he lives. I love that he's close to me.

Attempting my homework is pointless. Not because it's hard. It never is. Although I have to say, things are more challenging here. These teachers clearly put a lot of time into their lessons and homework, whereas my old teachers would hand out copies of some ancient worksheet and call it a day. The homework trauma I'm currently experiencing is that I can't concentrate on anything long enough to finish it. All I can think about is Scott. Wondering what's wrong with him. Wondering if I can help.

Maybe I should write him a warm fuzzy.

When Sadie told me about warm fuzzies, she sounded like one of those delusional idealists who think they can change the world. But I'm realizing that doing something nice for someone could be all about them. That's what it means to care about someone, even someone you don't know.

I call April and tell her about the warm-fuzzy thing.

"So do you think I should write Scott one?" I say.

"I don't see why not. It would be cute!"

"Are you sure it wouldn't be dorky?"

"Cute annihilates dorky."

"So it *is* dorky."

"Since when do you worry so much about what anyone thinks? The Brooke I know does her own thing, no matter what."

The Old Me that April knows is stuck back in New Jersey, longing for a better life. The New Me in New York is making that life happen. I'm taking more risks. I'm putting myself out there. There's a lot more to worry about.

"Did I tell you I turned down Robby Miller?" April says.

"No! When?"

"Yesterday."

How could she not have told me this yesterday? We always tell each other everything right away.

"What did you say?" I ask.

"Just that I'm not in a dating space right now."

"What's a *dating space*?"

"Something I made up so I wouldn't sound like a horrible person?"

"You're not horrible."

"Oh, no? Tell that to Robby Miller."

"We can't help who we like. Or don't like."

"I'm never going to have a boyfriend." April sounds defeated.

"Of course you will," I assure her. "You're just surrounded by idiots is all. It has nothing to do with you."

"Blerg. Mom's shouting at me to set the table. I'd better go."

"OK. Don't worry about Robby. He'll get over it. When he's, like, thirty."

"Write that warm fuzzy already!"

April is right. It's time to stop thinking and start doing.

Walking down Scott's street is so much better now that I know where I'm going. I tape the warm fuzzy under his doorbell. Then I practically run home so I can't change my mind about leaving it. I used this piece of cherry-red stationery I found mixed in with all my other paper. I can't remember where it came from. It's like that red paper was waiting for the day when it would serve a vital purpose. I used a black metallic pen to write:

Scott—
I'm here if you need me.
Thinking of you . . .
—Brooke

I really wanted to write "*Love, Brooke,*" but that might have scared him off. I considered using a cute "*xo*" like Sadie does. That didn't seem to fit, either. In the end I just signed my name, hoping Scott wouldn't think I'm a total dork.

Scott doesn't think I'm a total dork. Or if he does, he's hiding it well.

"It was really nice of you to leave that note," he says in class the next day. "Thanks."

"You're welcome. It's this random acts of kindness thing I'm doing with Sadie." OK, where did that come from? The goal was for Scott to think I'm *not* a dork.

Note to self: invent verbal delete button.

Scott opens his Dunder Mifflin notebook. But we don't need to take notes today because we have a sub. Mr Peterson left some fun optical-illusion stuff we're supposed to work on in pairs.

Scott and I scrunch our desks closer. We finish the sheet in fifteen minutes. Then we have the rest of the class free.

"Can you make a dragon?" Scott says.

"What?"

"An origami dragon."

"Please. Give me something hard to make." I rummage through the papers stuck in Scott's notebook until I find a bowling-team flyer. "Can I use this?"

"You can rip out a new sheet."

"I only use found paper. It's more challenging that way."

"Didn't you use a new sheet when you made that cup?"

"Only because he was drinking from it."

Scott watches as I fold the paper into a dragon. Dragons are a lot easier to make than they look. You're supposed to glue the head on at the end. Instead, I get some tape from Mr Peterson's desk. The sub barely notices, immersed in *People*.

"How did you do that?" Scott says when I present his dragon. "You didn't even need a diagram."

"I've seen the diagram."

"But how can you remember everything?"

I'm not about to tell him how. That's one secret I'm determined to keep.

"I just do," I say. "What are you naming him?"

"Snuffleupagus."

"Good one."

"We had a dog named Snuffleupagus."

"Did you name him?"

"Yeah. We had to put him down."

"Aw."

"It was a long time ago. I was seven."

I push the dragon across Scott's notebook.

"Is he going to start breathing fire?" he asks.

"No. He's a friendly dragon."

"A friendly dragon. I like those."

"I knew you did, so. . ."

"Can you teach me how to make one?"

"Have you done origami before?"

"Never."

"Well, then we should probably start with a crane."

"Cranes are good."

"But only if you teach me how to do that flippy-twirly thing you do with your pen."

Scott laughs. He's laughing because I made him laugh. That's hot.

"Deal," he says.

I teach Scott a few basic folds. He's already lost. I try to show him the crane, but it's hard for him. He keeps making these uneven folds, like he can't tell where the crease divisions should go.

"No worries," I say. "It took me for ever to learn." This is not true. Origami came naturally to me.

"Moving on!" Scott grabs his pen. "The secret? Is all in the thumb."

It must be a pretty big secret. Because after Scott patiently demonstrates his technique and I fling my pen across the room twice, it becomes glaringly obvious that I'm not going to get how to do the flippy-twirly thing anytime soon. The second pen-flinging incident is particularly alarming. I'm trying to twirl my pen using the same smooth, quick motion that Scott uses, when it suddenly zings all the way over to Mr Peterson's desk, narrowly missing the sub's leg. She looks up from her magazine all dazed, as if she forgot that she was, in fact, in a classroom surrounded by students.

I decide it might be better to practice at home.

It's interesting how something that comes so easily

to one person can be so impossible for someone else. Not that I'm surprised any more. I've seen it my whole life. I knew I was different from the other kids all the way back in kindergarten. This psychologist used to take me into another room so she could "get to know me". Even though I was only four, I knew that was code for being tested. There were some logic problems and inkblot interpretations and a bunch of other tests I don't remember. Every time she came to get me, I was reminded of how different I was. All I wanted to do was fit in. Even back then I downplayed my capabilities, trying to hide who I really was from the other kids so they'd like me.

Of course people found out eventually. You can't keep your true self hidden for ever, no matter how hard you try. I don't think any of it ever registered with Scott. Our school was enormous and we only had one class together. By that point I excelled at being invisible. Teachers were so disappointed with me that they didn't bother saying anything in class. They'd try to talk to me privately and then get discouraged when I didn't respond the way they wanted. But in elementary school, teachers would make comments about how smart I was and suddenly the whole class would be staring at me. They all had the same expression. Part intimidation, part jealousy. But mostly they were freaked out.

I never want anyone to look at me that way again. If it means trying to hide who I am, I can live with that. Blending in is way easier than dealing with the consequences.

THIRTEEN

Espresso Boy is staring at me again.

He doesn't want me to know this. Every time I catch him looking at me, he looks away. Or he pretends that he's looking at the Joe shirts on the wall behind me.

He's kind of cute. I might even go and talk to him if I were interested. In my experience, it pays to be straightforward. Guys get totally flattered when they know you like them. Only, he's not the one I want to flatter.

Sadie told me she'd meet me here after school. She's late. I've been trying to avoid eye contact with Espresso Boy for longer than I care to admit. He's making it impossible for me to read my book. Either I feel him staring at me or I'm paranoid that he might be staring at me. When I go up to the counter for a snack, he's clearly not focused on his laptop the way he's pretending to be.

Right when I'm about to call Sadie, my phone rings.

"I'm *so* sorry," Sadie goes. "Mr Peterson caught me before I left and would not stop talking. I'm on my way."

"Actually, can we meet somewhere else?"

"Why?"

"He's here again," I whisper.

"Espresso Boy?"

"Yes."

"Could he be any more obvious?"

"Not really, no. Where are you?"

It's amazing how much my attitude toward Sadie has changed in only three weeks. I went from thinking we could never be friends to hanging out after school with her. We mostly talked about tutoring at first, but I can already feel a shift in our conversations. It started the day Sadie avoided Carlos at Rite Aid. Something about sharing her secret made us instantly closer. Part of me is relieved to have a friend here, even though I wasn't looking for one.

Fifteen minutes later, we meet up on the corner of Greenwich and Charles streets. We've already dumped our bags at home so they won't weigh us down.

"This," Sadie says, "is my favourite walk." We go down Charles Street on Sadie's preferred side. It's a route that's already familiar to me. When I go to the park by myself, I usually chill in the Zen garden or just watch the city lights. But this time, we turn left and keep walking along the river.

"Mr Peterson loves you," she says. "You're like all he could talk about."

"Seriously?"

"We're both admirers of your big brain."

"Stop."

"Come on. You know it's true. Why don't you just admit you're a genius already?"

A shard of panic stabs my chest. "Did Mr Peterson tell you that?"

"Tell me what?"

"Nothing. Can we not talk about school?"

"Kitchenette is down here," Sadie offers. "We should go sometime. Their cupcakes rival Crumbs."

"I'm in."

"So I went back to Rite Aid."

"When?"

"Yesterday."

"Did you ask him out?"

"No, I didn't ask him *out*. I could hardly even look at him."

"What better way to gain boy confidence than to ask one out?"

"That's easy for you to say. You're gorgeous."

"Did you have a side of demented for lunch?"

"If I looked like you, I wouldn't have a problem asking anyone out."

Why Sadie has such low self-esteem is beyond me. Was she rejected by a boy before? Did she have a bad experience with someone she loved, like I did?

Sadie's right about this walk we're on. It's amazing. Not because of any one thing. It's more like the synergy of the water and the buildings and the streetlights and the people. All of it's making me feel overwhelmed.

There's something about the energy that's evoking all of the emotions I felt back home, wanting to be here so desperately. The deep sense of desire. The longing for the excitement and passion of city life. And it's different from walking by myself. Sharing this with Sadie somehow makes the experience more intense, even though she doesn't know how much it means to me. I hope this rush of finally getting to be a part of everything I dreamed about never goes away.

We pass an old paper factory with faded lettering. I love discovering buildings that used to be something else. It's sweet how they can have the chance to reinvent themselves.

"That's so cool," I say.

"What?"

"That building. See how it says it used to be a paper factory?"

"Oh. Yeah, that is cool."

"And that water tower over there."

"You look at water towers?"

"Of course. I love them."

"Why?"

"I just think they're beautiful."

"Oh. I've never noticed."

I remember the first time I saw Ree sketching. I was so jealous that she'd been living here her whole life surrounded by the energy and lights and buildings. But maybe those things are like background noise if you're from here. Maybe you have to experience this as a whole new place to appreciate it the way I do. Unless you're John. But he's not like anyone else.

"It's cool how you can do that," Sadie says. "It's like you only see the good parts of the city."

"It's amazing what you see when you look up."

"I guess I'm too busy looking down. Don't want to step in anything."

"Ew."

"Harsh, but true."

"Well, I've wanted to live here for a really long time. I'm sort of . . . infatuated."

"I didn't know that."

"You're the first person I've told here." I don't know if it's this amazing walk or having an unexpected new friend or all the excitement of everything that's happened since I got here. I just suddenly want to tell Sadie why I'm here. I want to share it with someone who isn't scandalized by my decision like Candice or stuck in the middle like April. I took this huge, life-altering leap without really being able to experience it with anyone.

But I can't tell her yet. Scott has to be the first to know. And hopefully, he'll like what he hears.

FOURTEEN

When Mr Peterson asks me to stay after class, I immediately know what it's about. I can tell by the way he looks at me when he says we need to talk. It's the same look my old teachers got when they found out about me. I was hoping to avoid all that here. Why can't I just be the new girl, stopping by for senior year without all the pressure?

"Why didn't you tell me that you're a genius?" Mr Peterson wants to know.

"I'm really not."

"Your IQ is well above the genius level. That makes you a genius."

I stare at a broken piece of chalk on the floor. When Mr Peterson gets amped over whatever he's putting on the board, the chalk goes flying.

"How did you find out?" I ask.

"I've become increasingly fascinated by you." He leans back against the board, which is always a mistake for him. Mr Peterson is one of those teachers who have perpetual chalk dust on their butt. "Your logic skills are the most impressive I've ever seen, and I've been teaching longer than you've been alive. You're able to remember an incredible amount of detail after being exposed to something only once. All of your work is outstanding. I wanted to know more about your background, so I checked your file."

"You checked my *file*?"

"Teachers are allowed to do that."

He may be right, but that doesn't make me feel any less violated.

"I also asked your other teachers about you." My face must be giving away my rage because he quickly adds, "It's my responsibility to confirm that all of my tutors are maintaining at least an eighty-five average. You're the only one who's not. At this point in the marking period your average is seventy-three. You and I both know it should be a lot higher."

Even though this school is more challenging than my old one, I can still put in minimal effort and get passing grades. I study a little for tests and get high scores on those, so everything else just averages out in the C range.

My standard procedure for enduring these I'm So Disappointed in You lectures is to tune out and let whatever adult is on my case talk at me. I've perfected the technique after tolerating way too many speeches from my mom. And my old teachers. And assorted administrative types. Like it's some big crime to choose how you want to live your life while you're in high school.

I can't believe I have to hear all of this crap again. It's bad enough when kids have attitude in class just because I'm the only one who understands what the teacher is talking about or I remember some random piece of information from a reading. It's not like I've ever flaunted any of this. It's just the opposite. Life is so much easier when you get along with people, when you can fit in instead of being labeled as a freak. And once teachers know the truth, they expect tons more from me. The last thing I want to do is a bunch of extra work. So I've always downplayed my talents. Like when we took those IQ tests in eighth grade. April told me her IQ, but when she asked me what mine was I reduced it. By a lot.

"I'm doing OK in your class," I remind him.

"True. But I'm guessing that's because my class has a creative aspect to it that motivates you to work harder."

He's right, of course. Not that I'm admitting anything. In an interrogation, saying less is always best.

"So here's what I want to know," Mr Peterson says. "Why aren't you doing the kind of work that everyone knows you can do with half your brain tied behind your back?"

I don't know why, but my determination to tune out during another speech on how much I'm disappointing the world is crumbling. If I have to sit through one more of these, I swear I'm going to lose it. It's really annoying how Mr Peterson went poking around in my file, sticking his nose where it doesn't belong. Why can't he just leave me alone?

"The work," I explain, "is part of a system with which I do not agree."

"Which system is that?"

"The public school system."

"Ah." He nods up at the ceiling. "It does have a lot of problems, doesn't it?"

Wow. That's the first time I've heard a teacher come even remotely close to admitting that the system majorly sucks.

"What's the main problem, in your opinion?" he says.

"There are so many. But I think the biggest problem is that schools offer this dimwitted curriculum that couldn't be more boring and then teachers get mad when students aren't interested in their classes. It's so stupid."

"I've noticed that problem as well. That's why I created Outside the Box."

"This is the only interesting class I've ever taken. Classes like this didn't even exist at my old school."

"That's a shame."

"Schools teach to the test and then they make these sweeping judgments about students based on their answers to a few pointless questions that they're just going to forget after the test anyway. And they have the nerve to call that an education. They're doing it wrong." I should probably shut up, but my rage is boiling. "How is force-feeding us stuff that we don't care about making us smarter? And why should I be forced to become part of something I don't believe in? Like, what, just because I'm capable, it automatically means I have to play into a corrupt system? I know you're disappointed in me, but I'm disappointed in the quality of education we're being offered. Doesn't *that* matter?"

The expression on Mr Peterson's face is hard to read at first. But then I think I recognize it.

It's respect.

For the first time in the history of us, talking to April is hard. Talking to April shouldn't be anywhere near hard. I can't figure out what's wrong. When I moved we promised to talk every day, which we did for the first couple of weeks. Then things shifted. There wasn't any dramatic change or anything. It was probably imperceptible at first, already happening before I noticed. But today, it's obvious.

The weirdness starts when I ask April if she thinks Candice will ever talk to me again.

"I don't know," April says.

I wait for her to continue. She doesn't.

"Well, is she still insanely mad at me?" I ask. "Or just kind of mad?"

"I'd say she's still insanely mad."

"Does she talk about me?"

"You really need to stop asking me about Candice."

"Why?"

"Because it's not fair to put me in the middle."

"But you see Candice every day. I moved away, remember?"

"Oh, *I* remember. Maybe you should remember, too."

"What's that supposed to mean?"

"Remember how Candice liked Scott? And how you knew that but you went after him anyway?"

"But that was so long ago! And he didn't even like her back!"

"It doesn't matter. You knew that she liked him and you went after him anyway. How did you think that would make her feel?"

"Are you on her side or something?"

April sighs. "I'm not on anyone's side. I'm just saying."

"Because it sounds like you're on her side."

This is so ridiculous. Candice got mad because I followed Scott here. I get that. But is she going to stay mad for ever? How long will it take before we can move on?

As if my day wasn't stressful enough. I'm still pissed at Mr Peterson for getting in my face. I guess it could have been worse, though. If I'd vented my anti-corrupt-system opinions to any other teacher, they probably would have suspended me. It feels so good to be not only understood but also listened to. It really seemed like Mr Peterson sympathized with what I was saying. But then he said that if I don't get my average up to 85, I'd be kicked out of tutoring.

"It's the rule," he threw down.

"Some rules are meant to be broken," I countered.

"Nice try. You have three weeks to get your average up or you won't be tutoring with us any more."

Like I care. Tutoring wasn't something I wanted to do anyway. I just joined to get Sadie off my back. So what if I get kicked out? There are plenty of other people who could help John. OK, maybe not plenty, but there has to be someone.

"I'm sorry if you feel like you're stuck in the middle," I tell April. "I'm just trying to ask about Candice."

"Well, don't. When she's ready to talk to you, she will."

I've been cleaning my room the whole time we've been talking. My bag is a mess. I turn it over on my bed and shake everything out. Then I find his note.

"Oh my god," I say.

"What?"

"I think Scott wrote me a note. I just found it in my bag." But reality sets in when I realize that my name isn't written in his handwriting. I don't recognize the writing at all.

"What does it say?"

I open it. My heart sinks. I was still hoping it could be from Scott.

"It's from Espresso Boy."

"From the coffeehouse?"

"Yeah. He must have snuck it into my bag yesterday when I got up for a snack. He put his number in it."

"Are you going to call him?"

"I don't think so. No. Calling him to say I like

someone else would be cruel. It would be worse than not calling. Don't you think?"

"Are you sure you don't like him?"

"Um, I moved here for Scott?"

Silence. April and I would normally analyze some boy liking one of us for hours. But things are so tense that I can tell this part of the conversation is over.

"So," I say. "What else is going on with you?"

"You know, same old around here. Everyone's totally over school and it's not even October. I don't know how we're going to survive until June."

"It's like that here, too."

"Is it? I thought your new school was so much better."

"It is. But the kids act pretty much the same."

"What happened today? You said some teacher made you stay after. . . ?"

"Oh, yeah. Mr Peterson." I tell April what happened. "Can you believe he's making me do actual work?"

"He's not making you. You could always quit tutoring, right?"

"Yeah. I'm considering it. But then Sadie would get on my case again and I really don't need the stress."

"Why do you care if some girl is bothering you about tutoring? Just say you don't want to do it."

"I tried that. She's relentless. And Sadie's not just some girl. She's my friend."

More silence.

"You still there?" I ask.

"This might be a good thing. Doing work, I mean."

"Why? You know I don't agree with the system."

"Yeah, but why does that mean you can't take advantage of it?"

"Like how?"

"Like rocking your transcript so you can go to a good college."

"I think it's too late for that. We have to start applying soon."

"Too bad you wasted all those years," she says. "You could have gone to Harvard or Yale."

"What for? I don't even know what I want to do with my life."

"No offense? But maybe it's time you started figuring that out."

"You know it's not that simple."

"You want to hear something simple? You could have had straight As with like no effort. You could have been valedictorian. But you threw it all away, and for what? To make some kind of radical statement no one's listening to? To prove some point no one's benefiting from? Wake up, Brooke. No one cares."

April's never been like this. I don't know what's going on, but I don't like it.

"Where's all this coming from?" I ask.

"Do you have any idea how hard it is for the rest of us? Every college I'm interested in wants me to be smarter or more involved in activities or more unique or just . . . *more*. If I had what you have, any one of them would take me with no problem. You have this amazing gift and you're totally wasting it."

I've heard this countless times before. From my mom, from teachers, from guidance counsellors, from pretty much every adult who feels like they have a say in the kind of person they think I should be. But coming from April, the message has a whole new meaning.

Unbelievable. April is one of them and I didn't even know it.

Or maybe she only started feeling this way after I left. People can get a little crazy when someone they care about leaves. Even if she's been feeling this way for a long time, keeping it bottled up inside, there's a reason it's coming out now. She doesn't seem worried that what she's saying is hurtful. Which concerns me. Because what if the distance between us is bigger than our friendship?

How do you stay best friends with someone when you're living in two different worlds?

FIFTEEN

The small group that Sadie tutors in English just received a fresh batch of warm fuzzies. Sadie was working on them while we were on the phone last night. She called me for help with a calc problem and then we just kept talking. Sadie said how she wants everyone she tutors to be encouraged (if they're struggling) or rewarded (if they're improving) by a sparkly, personalised warm fuzzy. Watching Sadie hand them out, it's obvious that everyone thinks they're the cutest things ever.

John and I are at our usual table. Since it's raining, there's no High Line for us today. John threw a minor tantrum over it. He hates when we have to stay in. Even his shirt is angry. It has a stick figure throwing a tizzy fit and underneath it says: IT'S ALWAYS SOMETHING.

"Why does it have to rain today?" he complains. "Out of all the possible non-tutoring days to rain. It's so *unfair*."

"The High Line will still be there," I assure him.

"That's what's so frustrating. It's out there taunting us with its existence."

One of the girls in Sadie's group squeals. She gets up and hugs Sadie.

John glances at them. "Wonder what that's about."

"Sadie's giving out warm fuzzies."

"Warm what now?"

"They're these little notes that are supposed to make you happy. Sadie's giving them to everyone in her group."

John's mouth falls open. "How come you never give me any warm fuzzies?"

"I didn't know you wanted any."

"Consider yourself notified."

"Well then, I promise to deliver."

As usual, it's a challenge keeping John focused on work. I can tell that he really wants to improve, it's just hard for him to concentrate on any one thing for more than a few minutes. Especially when we're working inside. Out on the High Line, the buzzing city energy seems to soothe him. Which I totally understand because I'm the same way.

"How can you be so extraordinary in every single subject?" John wants to know.

"Trust me, I'm not."

"Uh, yeah you are. You're like the academic polar opposite of me." He picks up his history test again, miserably shaking his head at it. The red *61* scrawled on top glares back at him. "I'm sure you've never got a D in your life. Or even a B."

"Actually, I've got lots of them. Even zeroes."

"Seriously?"

"Yep."

"But . . . why?"

"You got a D, too. Ds happen."

"But they shouldn't happen to you. You can ace anything you want."

"Key word being *want*. I don't want to live in some bubble, doing homework and studying and caring about classes. It's not my style."

John is agog.

"What?" I go.

He doesn't say anything, just miserably shakes his head some more. It's so weird. First Mr Peterson, then April, and now John. Did they somehow plan to gang up on me?

After we do some trig, John's like, "What do you want to be when you grow up?"

"I don't know."

More miserable head shaking.

"Why?" I ask. "Do you?"

"Of course," he informs me in a duh tone. "I'm going to be a social worker so I can help kids like me."

John is the last person I expected to have such conviction about his career path. I assumed he'd slack off at some community college for a while, if that. Now I'm embarrassed that I judged him so harshly.

I'm actually kind of jealous. I'd love to have that same certainty, that same "*I'm going to be*," which is even more solid than the typical "*I want to be.*" I hate not knowing what I want to do.

I want to know. I just don't know how to know.

I came here for you.

We belong together.

You're just starting to know me, but I'm already in love with you.

Ways to tell Scott why I'm here constantly invade my brain. They keep me up at night. They won't shut up until he knows the truth about us.

It's time.

Ever since our sandwich-shop interlude, it's been obvious that Scott and I have a connection. He must feel it, too. Because if two people have a real connection, how can it only be apparent to one of them? Another thing is that Leslie might be out of the picture. I saw them together after school the other day and she did not look happy. More important, neither did he.

After tutoring, Sadie asked me to go with her to Strawberry Fields tonight, that place in Central Park she was telling me about. It sounds very New York, so of course I told her I'd go. John overheard and said he wanted to come, too. I love how kids are so spontaneous here. Back home, everyone planned stuff way in advance. Here, the city is our playground and we can play whenever we want.

OK, maybe not *whenever* we want. Other people's

parents don't always let them go out. My dad hasn't said no to anything yet, though. He's usually not even home when I want to go somewhere, so I just leave him a note and go. Since he doesn't know how to do the parent thing, he's kind of treating me like an adult. Which I know I shouldn't complain about. But even though I'd never admit this to anyone, it's comforting to have rules sometimes.

I walk home down Scott's street, the way I usually go if I'm not doing something with Sadie after school. Every time I pass his building I look up and wonder which window is his.

This time he's sitting on the stoop, eating pretzels.

My heart slams against my chest.

"Hey, you," he says.

"Hey," I say.

"What's up?"

"Not much. We're going to Central Park later."

"Who's we?"

"Me and Sadie and John from tutoring. Do you want to come?"

"You're just going to hang out, or. . . ?"

"There's this place where people get together and play Beatles songs. It's right across from where John Lennon lived."

"Yeah?"

"Yeah. It sounds cool."

"It does sound cool. I'm in."

"Sweet," I say, hoping that I'm acting casual. This

is huge. Scott's coming with me. We can walk home together after. Then I'll finally tell him.

If I can avoid throwing up.

At six, Sadie and John are already waiting at the subway stop.

"Scott's coming with us," I tell them.

"Scott who?" John says.

"Scott Abrams. You probably don't know him — he's new."

"I know who he is. Isn't he from New Jersey?"

"Yeah."

"Isn't he from the same town you're from?"

"Um. Yeah."

"Hey, guys," Scott says, crossing the street. "Sorry I'm late."

"You're not," I tell him.

John stares at us.

"Let's go!" Sadie says, pulling on John's arm.

Strawberry Fields is too awesome for words. It's this little clearing surrounded by trees and benches. At the centre there's a tile mosaic on the ground that says IMAGINE. Bunches of flowers are scattered around it. People are everywhere — singing along with some guys playing "Hey Jude" on their guitars, posing next to the Imagine mosaic while their friends take pictures, or just passing through, absorbing the scene.

There's only one free bench. As we're going for it, I notice some girls coming at it from the opposite direction. I grab Sadie's arm and we run, hurling ourselves over the bench to save room for the boys. John comes crashing in next, forcing himself between us.

"Ow!" Sadie yells.

"Sorry!" John apologizes, bouncing back up.

Scott sits down where John just was. Since I'm smooshed up against this hippie dude on the next bench, the only space left for John is on the other side of Sadie.

Sadie wanted to come here today because it's John Lennon's birthday. Which is probably why it's so crowded. The biggest bunch of flowers has a giant card that says, "Happy Birthday, John. You will live for ever in our hearts." I wonder if someone comes by at night to take the cards and flowers away.

None of us really know any Beatles songs except for Sadie, but John and I sing along with some of the choruses. Scott doesn't sing at all.

"You don't know any of their songs?" I ask him.

"I know some. I just don't sing."

"Ever?"

"Never."

"Because . . . you don't like your voice?"

"It's more of a tone-deaf issue."

"That might improve with practise."

"Oh, I'm beyond hope."

John is belting out the chorus to "Let It Be" at the top of his lungs.

I move closer to Scott. Nothing is remotely as intense as being this close to him. "John doesn't let that stop him," I whisper.

Scott laughs. I love that he thinks I'm funny. I didn't even know anyone thought I was funny until Scott told me one time walking home. So of course now I'm always trying to think of ways to make him laugh.

"I'm having a Look Up moment," John broadcasts.

I see where he's looking. It's this amazing rooftop garden with trees and tall grasses like the kind in the Zen garden. He's waiting for confirmation that the rooftop is, in fact, amazing.

I'm still pressed up against Scott. It's impossible to focus on anything else.

The energy of this space is incredible. All of these people are gathered here for a common purpose: to worship at the altar of their musical religion. It's like we're sharing this secret realm for a while and then we'll return to our normal, less spectacular lives. You could totally walk by on the other side of the trees along Central Park West and not even notice this place. I'm realizing that New York is filled with all sorts of secluded enclaves where people get together to celebrate what makes them feel alive. These kinds of things didn't exist back home. Here, excitement never fades. It's like a drug.

"There's Danny!" Sadie yells. "I love that kid." She points to a boy about our age who's just tacked himself to the cluster of guitar players. Danny doesn't look as comfortable with his guitar as they do.

I lean over Scott's lap. "Who is he?" I ask Sadie.

"We met last time I was here. He was just learning

guitar and that was, like, right before summer. I can't believe how good he is already."

We all watch Danny. He drops his pick.

"Is this a love connection?" John wonders.

"What? No! He has a girlfriend. Anyway, he's not my type." Sadie throws me a sidelong glance.

I wish I could drag her into Rite Aid, shove her in front of Carlos, and force her to ask him out. As if I can talk. Here I am pressing up against Scott and whispering in his ear and he doesn't even know how I feel about him. I'm even more frustrating than she is. But only until I get Scott alone later.

When we leave, I strategize a way for me and Scott to walk home together.

"You guys going home?" I ask on our way to the subway.

"Unfortunately," Sadie says, "I still have to deal with calc. Can you believe our homework?"

I finished that homework really quickly. So I just make a face like, *Could Ms Jacobs be any more of a sadist?*

John pokes my arm. "It's a nice night for the High Line," he says. "Wanna go?"

I peek at Scott. I hope he didn't notice John poking me.

"Um. . ."

"No pressure, it's just that I'm going anyway – I mean, duh, I live there, but I'm staying out for a while."

"I would, but Sadie's right about our homework. It's impossible."

Both John and Sadie give me looks.

"What?" I go. "It is." That was stupid. I'm sure they know by now that I never think homework is impossible.

"Your loss," John taunts. "Let the record show that you are severely missing out."

On the subway ride downtown, I'm only half listening to the conversation, which is mostly between Sadie and John. Scott's been kind of quiet all night. I'm trembling with anticipation over my perfectly executed escape from all of us walking the same way when we get to our stop. John even gets out early at 23rd Street instead of 14th Street. After he steps off the train he tilts back in, blocking the doorway.

"Last chance!" he yells.

Out of everyone in the subway car who just heard John yell, only one person looks over.

"Rain check," I tell him.

"Promise?"

"Promise."

The closing-door signal dings. John flings himself away before the doors can crush him.

The walk to Scott's is a blur. I'm still trembling. I'm so nervous about what I'm going to say and how I'm going to say it. My mouth is all dry. I knew I should have got some water when we were leaving the park.

"Are you cold?" Scott asks.

"No, I'm OK." I could branch off and walk home a shorter way, but I told Scott I felt like walking some more.

When we get to his building, I have no idea how I'll even begin explaining myself.

"So . . . that was cool," I say. "Did you like it?"

"I really did. Sorry if I seemed out of it."

"No, you weren't. . ."

We're just hovering there on his stoop with Scott standing a step above me and me leaning against the railing. I try to picture us as if this were a scene from a movie, one where the perfect romantic ending is just about to be filmed. This is the part where the girl tells the boy she's in love with him and the boy says something like, "What took you so long?" And then they have their first kiss, the one you've been waiting for the whole time, and it's just as perfect as you hoped it would be.

I take a breath to let the scene begin.

"It's just that . . . we have some issues," Scott goes. "Family stuff. Something happened right before I met up with you guys."

"Oh."

"It's my brother. Ross. He's . . . an alcoholic."

Holy crap. Is Scott Abrams actually telling me this?

"He's away at college. Or he was. He dropped out. Stopped going to class, that sort of thing. He tries to hold down random jobs, but he always loses them. Goes on these heavy benders. Stops showing up." Scott scuffs his shoe against the stair. "Then he calls my mom for money. She used to send him some, but now my dad is done. He totally cut Ross off, told him not to call us any more."

"That's . . . oh my god."

"None of us knows what to do. Ross won't go to rehab. He's never lasted more than a few weeks in AA. I'm the only one who still talks to him. I don't want to, I just . . . feel like I have to. You know?"

I nod.

"So that's how I know what's going on with him. He just lost another job."

"Is that why you get . . . like, sometimes you get kind of sad and quiet at school. Is that why?"

"Yeah. I can't really deal with anything after I talk to him." Scott rakes his fingers through his hair, looking down the street. "OK, I didn't mean to dump all that on you. You must be like—"

"No! Are you kidding? I'm the one who asked you what was wrong, remember?"

"Thanks for listening and . . . everything. I've never told anyone about Ross. I guess I really needed to vent."

"Totally. You can vent to me anytime."

He smiles sadly. "I know I can trust you with this."

"Everything stays between us."

We sit in silence on his stoop, watching people go by and lights blinking on behind windows. I think we both feel like it would seem weird for me to walk away after everything he said. So I sit next to him, letting him know I'll always be there for him, without having to say a word.

SIXTEEN

It's getting cold. I knew I should have put a scarf in my bag before I left for school this morning. That's what Sadie would have done. She always says how I should check the forecast every morning, but I really can't be bothered.

"So how'd your homework go?" John says.

"Hm?" I take a few books and a notebook out of my bag, stacking them on the big lounge bench we always try to get whenever we come out to the High Line. I might have a cardigan shoved in here somewhere.

"That calc homework you had to do instead of hanging out with me?"

"I finished it."

"I'm sure you did."

There's no cardigan anywhere in my bag. It's freaking cold.

Note to self: always bring a cardigan.

"Did you get your trig test back?" I ask.

"We were supposed to, but Richards still hasn't graded them. You are so lucky you don't have to deal with remedial mathematics."

"Oh, it's bad all over. Trust me."

"Why do you hate school so much?"

Even though my hatred for school isn't exactly a secret, no one's ever asked me where it came from before. It's always just been a given because everyone else hates school, too.

"Doesn't everybody?" I go.

"Pretty much, but that's because they struggle with it. You don't."

"We all do."

"Not you. Seriously, has any class ever been hard for you?"

I rub my arms, trying to generate some heat. "Where's all this coming from?"

John looks at me. He looks at me for so long that I start to get uncomfortable.

"Nowhere," he says. "Forget it."

"Do you have a problem with me tutoring you because I don't get better grades?"

"Hardly. You're the first tutor I've had where I feel like I'm actually getting the help I need. And if anyone's had way too many tutors, it's me. Do you know how lucky I am that I found you?"

Old Me would have played it off like what he just said was nothing. But New Me thinks what John said is sweet.

"Thanks," I tell him.

We work for a while so I can tell Mr Peterson that we're not slacking when we're out here. I want to find a way to explain John's homework so he really understands it. Sometimes he says he gets it, but then he forgets everything at home.

John always asks a million questions. At first, this was extremely annoying. But now I admire him. He's so motivated. Despite his problems concentrating and how hard writing is for him, he never gives up. His career goal is so important to him that nothing can stand in his way.

"You're going to be a really good social worker," I say.

John looks up from his worksheet. He smiles at me. I smile back, shivering.

"Here," he says. He takes off his black hoodie and gives it to me. "Put this on." He's wearing a plain grey T-shirt over a white thermal. I didn't know he had any plain T-shirts.

"Won't you be cold?"

"Dude. I live right over there. If I'm cold, I'll just go get another one."

He's not kidding. John has an extensive hoodie collection.

I put the hoodie on. It's really soft inside.

"Better?" John asks.

"Much."

"Can you believe we've been here, like, five times and we've never noticed the best water tower?"

"I noticed it. I told you last time. Or the time before that."

"I don't think so."

"Remember how you were all, 'The fat water tower rules!' and I kept arguing that the skinny one was better?"

"And then you agreed with me about the fat one? Yeah, I remember."

"No I didn't."

"Oh, I think you did."

"Well, you're thinking wrong."

"Way to be a supportive tutor. How much are they paying you again?"

"Hilarious."

"Seriously, though. Look up."

If I don't look up, John will keep yammering about this for ever. I look up. "What, that little one? He's cute, but kind of average."

"Not him." John leans over behind me and points so I can see exactly where he means. "Him." He appears to be pointing at a massive water tower, all hunkered down overlooking the river.

"That's an old one." It's this ancient, dark metal thing. It looks like a shadow of itself.

"Wait for it," John says.

"For what?"

"It."

A few minutes later, the sun slips behind the water tower. The effect is like a total solar eclipse, with the water tower blocking the sun. Light radiates outward in rays of bright red and orange.

"Whoa."

"Thanks, I arranged that myself."

"How did you know that was going to happen?"

"When you've spent as much time looking out your window as I have, you notice everything." John checks his watch. "Four thirty-seven. Right on time for October tenth."

The things John puts up with at school must be seriously hard to handle. I know how harsh kids can be around someone they think is "slow". I've heard the comments in class when teachers call on a kid who never gets it. And we've all seen kids who are different being tormented. John's never said anything to me, but I can tell he endures way more than he reveals. It bothers me that people judge him. But what I hate the most is that I used to be one of them. I saw the way he struggled to do even the easiest worksheets and I assumed he wasn't smart. But that's so not true. John is smarter than most people I know.

"We can get up there," John says, "if you want."

"Where?"

"That roof. Then you could see the water tower up close. It's amazing – it even has a ladder you can climb up."

"I love rooftops."

"Of course you do. So . . . you ready?"

We go. John navigates the way down some zigzag streets, pointing out polished wooden garage doors that used to be stable entrances and buildings that once had fallout shelters. Then he says, "This is it."

This can't be it. I was expecting some run-down tenement with an unlocked back door we could sneak in. The building we're in front of is totally renovated. It's all glass and wood with a fancy lobby and doorman. There's no way they'll let us in.

John rings one of the doorbells, waving to the doorman. The doorman waves back.

"You know the doorman?" I ask.

"I have connections."

Someone who's not the doorman comes out. He's an older guy wearing a brown work shirt and jeans. A ratty blue cloth is sticking out of his back pocket. There's a huge ring of keys clamped to his belt loop.

"How's it going, John?" he says.

"It's all good. Elias, this is Brooke. Brooke, this is my friend Elias."

"Hi," I say.

"Nice to meet you," Elias says, holding the door open for us. Then he puts us in the elevator. We're allowed to take it up to the roof.

"How do you know Elias?"

"He used to be our super. I think this is a better gig for him. He gets his own apartment here, rent free."

One cool thing about John is that his friends are mostly older people from around the neighbourhood. It took me a while to figure out who his friends were because I usually don't see him with anyone at school. I think having grownups for friends gives you this worldly aura. When we have tutoring, John usually tells me about some fascinating thing one of his friends did. I really look forward to his stories.

The roof is beyond incredible. I can't even believe it. There are enormous trees up here. And tables and chairs and flowers and even sections of grass designed to look like an upscale yard or something. But this is way better than a yard. From up here, you can see everything. Streetlights and pavements and people and tons of other buildings. I could stay up here for ever watching the city breathe below us, watching night turn into day and back into night again.

"This is amazing," I gape.

"Thank you, thank you, no autographs, please." John grabs my hand. "Come here."

We go over to the edge of the roof, which is bordered by a cement wall. The wall is the perfect height to lean against without feeling like you're going to fall over. So I lean against it, looking down at the streets. Distant traffic noises float up. I look out over the river to the place I'm from, feeling this nostalgic tug. Not that I want to move back or anything. It's just that part of me will always be there.

I used to have these intense dreams where I watched the New York City skyline shining in the night. In this one dream I kept having, I'd get up in the middle of the night, go over to the window, and pull the curtain aside. A wall of buildings would be right there, all huge, a million lit windows glimmering at me. It was all so close, yet so far away.

And now I'm here. And the energy is waking me up.

"You're quiet," John says.

"I'm in awe."

"That's how I was the first time I came up here. I stayed all night to watch the sunrise."

"Shut up! I was just thinking that!"

"We can do it anytime you want."

"Your mom lets you stay out all night?"

"I'm sure she'd make an exception. I wasn't entirely honest with her last time. I think I said I was staying over at a friend's. What about your dad? Would he let you stay out?"

"Like he'd even notice." I rip my eyes away from the view to look at John, who's leaning against the wall next to me. "I've always wanted to live here."

"Word?"

"Yeah, for a long time."

"Is that why you moved?"

How am I supposed to answer that? I mean, it is and it isn't. If I didn't want to live in New York so much, would I have followed Scott here?

"Not exactly," I say.

John doesn't push me to explain. He says, "You're different now from when you first got here. You were. . . It's like you're softer or something."

"Thanks a lot!"

"You know you had an edge when we first met. Now it's not as sharp."

He's right. It's the energy. All of this possibility makes me want to be a better person.

Back in New Jersey, I never felt like I was really home. I was restless for the excitement of city life. Now I'm surrounded by everything I wished for. And best of all, I feel like I've finally found where I belong.

SEVENTEEN

The call from Mom goes like this.

Mom: How are your grades?

Me: I told you. We don't get report cards until next week.

Mom: That's no reason not to know how you're doing. Can't you ask your teachers?

Me: [exasperated sigh] No one does that. Teachers don't want to be bothered.

Mom: It's not a bother. It's their job.

Me: I'll just wait for my report card.

Mom: You must have some idea of how you're doing. Didn't you say you're a tutor now? Aren't there grade requirements for that?

Me: Yes, and I'm getting my grades up, so—

Mom: Up from what?

Me: [pause] The first marking period wasn't the best.

Mom: How bad was it?

Me: Not great.

Mom: First you tell me you want to move because

a better academic environment would motivate you. Now you're telling me a different story.

Me: [silence]

Mom: Next you're going to tell me that living with your father is working out.

Me: It's fine.

Mom: [snorts] Somehow I find that hard to believe.

There's no way I'm telling her the truth about me and Dad. All of the hurt that lies underneath the glossy surfaces of my new room. All of the things we don't say, covered by polite conversation.

We're all hiding something. Even Scott's family, which seems completely standard from the outside, has a burning secret. There's a reason that out of all the people he could have told, he told me about Ross. Scott knows he can trust me. He needs me just as much as I need him. I want him to know that I'll always be here for him. That we can help each other in ways no one else can.

That we belong together.

I take out my wish box and read all of the notes I've written to myself. Most of these were written way before I got here. And now here I am. With Scott right down the street. Part of me wants to keep why I'm here a secret and just see how things develop between us. I'm really afraid to tell him. I'm afraid that he won't feel the same way and then we won't even be friends. But then I remember The Knowing.

Now more than ever, I know that we belong together.

Suddenly, I'm overcome by this sense of urgency. I can't leave my room fast enough. I run out with that electrifying Friday-night feeling pushing me forward. Slicing through the night down his street with my heart racing. All that matters is finally being together.

When I get to his block, I slow down. I smooth my hair. I attempt to regulate my breathing.

I ring his bell.

My heart speeds up again. I take a few deep breaths.

"Who is it?" his voice crackles over the intercom.

"It's me, Brooke."

The door buzzes to let me in. Except I can't go in. His parents are probably home. There's no way I can say what I have to say in front of them. One thing about New York apartments is that there's zero privacy. Even going to the bathroom without everyone knowing your business is a challenge. I can't risk telling Scott in his room anyway. What if he doesn't feel the same way? Being able to escape quickly is essential.

I ring his bell again.

"Is the door not working?" Scott crackles.

"Can you come down?"

"Oh, yeah. Give me a minute."

Fabulous. I probably interrupted a profound conversation he was having with Leslie. She might even be up there with him. Maybe I should leave. I could always tell him I forgot that I had to be somewhere.

Scott opens the door. My stomach turns over.

"Hey, neighbour," he says.

I open my mouth to say hi. Nothing comes out.

He's like, "What's up?"

This is it. This is the It that was supposed to be the It at the junior picnic last year. This is the It that's long overdue.

"Is Leslie your girlfriend?" I ask. I was not planning to start with that. It just came out.

"Not exactly," he says. "It's complicated."

"How complicated?"

Scott thinks. "Let's just say we're not looking at things the same way."

This could either be really good or really bad. Does he mean that he's the one who's more serious about things? Or that Leslie is? If I had to guess, I'd say that Leslie is the one who's more serious.

Let's hope I'm right.

"I came here for you," I say.

"Um ... yeah, cool. So did you want to get a sandwich, or. . . ?"

"No, I mean ... I came to New York for you. I moved here to be with you."

"You moved here for me?"

I nod.

"Why?"

"Because . . . OK, I know this sounds weird since we didn't even know each other before. But ... I just felt like if you got to know me, you'd see that we belong together."

146

"But we hardly know each other."

"No, I know. I know it's weird."

"Wow. That's . . . a lot."

"Sorry. I didn't mean to . . . overwhelm you."

"I don't know what to say."

"That's OK." Tears sting my eyes. "I'll just . . . I should go."

If Scott wants to be with me, he would be telling me right now. But he's not saying anything. He's just standing there. Looking anywhere but at me.

I.

Am.

Mortified.

"You don't have to go," Scott says.

"Yeah. I kind of do."

I cannot get home any faster. I want to run, but I'm crying. Running and crying don't mix very well. I learned that the hard way.

So this is what it feels like when your heart shatters.

I can't believe The Knowing betrayed me. Everything I thought was true is a lie. Not that I should be surprised. This being the story of my life and all.

It's hard to tell how much time has passed when you want the world to go away. I just want to hide out here in my room for ever. I've already cried through half a box of tissues. Dad not coming home until way later is a good thing this time.

The doorbell rings.

There's no way I can answer the door. I've been

crying so hard that my face is all puffy and my eyes are red. If I ignore whoever it is, they'll go away.

Except they don't. The doorbell keeps ringing. *So* irritating. Why can't they just leave me alone? What does everyone want from me?

When the doorbell rings for the billionth time, I pound down the stairs and yank the front door open, not even asking who it is.

It's Scott.

He doesn't say anything. He doesn't have to. He puts his arms around me and pulls me close to him.

And when he kisses me, every one of my wishes comes true.

EIGHTEEN

Scott Abrams kissed me last night.

I have to keep replaying the kiss to convince myself that it really happened. Not that I could think about anything else. Scott actually came over. Scott actually kissed me.

The Knowing was right all along.

After he kissed me, I didn't invite him in or anything. I was too overwhelmed by the enormity of it all to access my thinking skills. He just said, "See you tomorrow." Then I watched him walk away. Eventually, he turned to see if I was still there. I was. I could see his goofy smile from halfway down the block.

As if that weren't awesome enough? We're going out tonight. OK, it's not exactly a date. We're doing something for school. With Sadie and John. It's this project for the Box in which we're researching how knowledge of pop culture creates social bonds. I got the idea from John. He goes to trivia nights at this coffeehouse called The Situation Room. When John was telling me how his team couldn't get together for this month's trivia night and you need a minimum of four people to play, I thought it would be perfect if the four of us went as a team.

Sadie and I were supposed to walk over together, but she called to say she'd meet us there instead. She didn't say why. I'm hoping it's because she's at Rite Aid asking Carlos out. That would be hot because then we could double-date. But it's annoying because I wanted to tell her about Scott on the way there. It was too late to call her last night and I'm dying to tell her everything, starting from two years ago.

I'm already waiting on Scott's stoop when he comes out.

"Nice," he says.

Ever since Scott kissed me, I've been wondering when he's going to kiss me again. Actually, I've been more than wondering. I've been obsessing. It could be right now! In case it is right now, I've already crunched a bunch of mints. My breath is all tingly with spearminty freshness. The Situation Room is only like five blocks away. We don't have a lot of time if he wants to kiss me again before we get there. Or if he wants to hold my hand. Why isn't he trying to hold my hand?

"So," Scott says. "I'm glad you came over last night."

"I'm glad *you* came over."

"Yeah?"

"Totally."

"I just thought . . . when you told me about moving here and everything, that was . . . huge. No one's ever done anything like that for me."

"Well, I couldn't help it. I care about you."

"See, that amazes me. We didn't really know each other back home."

"You didn't know me at all."

"I knew you did origami."

"True."

"And I knew you were pretty."

"*Were* pretty?"

"*Are* pretty."

"Really?"

Scott looks at me. "Really." He brushes a wisp of hair away from my face. Which is almost as good as holding hands.

John saved a table for us. He's waving at us frantically, wedged between two crowded tables packed with rowdy trivia addicts.

"Do you see John anywhere?" Scott goes, trying not to smile.

John waves even more frantically.

"Who, John? Um, no. Why, is he here yet?"

"I don't think so."

We keep looking everywhere but at John. He's out of his chair now, narrowly missing some girl's head as his arm flies over her in desperation.

"Oh wait, there he is," I say.

"Funny," John snarks when we get to the table. "They weren't letting me hold the table any more. We could have lost it."

"Sorry," I tell him. "Are we late?"

John consults his watch. "Three minutes," he grumbles.

"Didn't know they were so strict," Scott says.

John's like, "Where's Sadie?"

"I don't know," I say. "But she told me she'd meet us here, so no worries."

"If she's not here in about two seconds we'll have to forfeit."

"Chill," Scott says. "She'll be here."

"But what if—"

Sadie bursts in, pushing her way toward us through the crowd. "Sorry, sorry! I was—"

"Welcome one and all to trivia night at The Situation Room!" the moderator booms into the mic. He's at a podium next to the front counter. The podium has a little reading light clamped to it. His stick-on name tag says, HI! MY NAME IS BILL. "My capable assistant, Amanda, will be coming around to register teams of four to six players. Four to six players, boys and girls! Be sure to get your team's answer form and pencils from her."

"What do you think the categories will be?" I ask John. I've heard so much about his trivia nights that I already know how they work. There are ten rounds of questions. Each round has its own category. Some categories are general, like Geography, while others are quirky specific, like European Castles. There are usually two pop-culture categories, which justifies using this for our project.

"Each round consists of ten questions, for a grand total of one hundred mind-bending mystifiers," Bill explains. "Anyone on your team can record your final answer on the answer form. Only answers on the answer form will be counted. If more than one answer is recorded in a response space, neither answer will be counted."

"What do we win?" some guy shouts from the back.

"Prizes!" Bill shouts back. "First prize is a round of free drinks for everyone on your team, plus everyone gets a Situation Room T-shirt!"

Hoots abound. What a bunch of geeks. Who else would get so excited about a low-rent shirt and some coffee?

"The runners-up will receive free drinks and Cracker Jack prizes!" Bill continues. "And third prize is a tasty snack."

"Do we have to split the snack?" the guy in the back shouts.

Bill's all, "Sounds like it's time to turn on those brain cells!"

John is excited. When John gets worked up, it's even harder for him to sit still. It's like all of his nervous energy whips up into a frenzy that's impossible to contain. He's jiggling his leg, which is making his chair rattle.

He passes our team answer form to me. "Want to do the honours? Write our names in?"

In the box at the top, I write:

Scott Abrams
Brooke Greene
Sadie Hall
John Dalton

"What do we put for our team name?" I ask John.

"What do you want to put?"

"I don't know. What's your regular team's name?"

"Endoplasmic Reticulum."

I look at Scott and Sadie. "What do you guys think it should be?"

"Blood Sugars?" Sadie suggests.

"Why?"

"Because I love that band. And it sounds cool."

"I think our name should have more significance," John says. "It should be something that describes all of us."

Scott goes, "So . . . what are we?"

That's a question I'm dying to ask him. Here we are, sitting with our friends who don't even know about us yet. Why isn't Scott telling them that we're together? Does he want to keep it a secret? He hasn't even touched me the whole time we've been here, except for one second when his elbow accidentally jabbed my arm.

"We're two New Yorkers and two New Jerseyans," Sadie decides.

"How about Two New?" Scott says.

John considers this. "Tell you what. Let's put that

down for now, and if we think of anything better we can change it."

"Works for me," I say, writing it in.

"First round!" Bill booms into the mic. The mic retaliates with a high-pitched whine of feedback. "The category is . . . Top Tens."

The first few questions are crazy obscure. John writes in a few answers. The rest of us are completely lost.

Then Bill goes, "Question four has two parts. Which eighties television show featured nightly top ten lists and what year did it premiere?"

"Letterman!" Sadie hisses.

"*The Late Show*," Scott adds, reaching for John's pencil.

"No!" I say too loudly. Then I hunch over the table. The tables are clustered so closely together that other teams could be spying on us. "It wasn't called that before," I explain, lowering my voice. "It was *Late Night with David Letterman*."

"Are you sure?" John asks.

"I own this one." I write it in, buzzing on adrenaline over knowing an answer. "It came on in 1982."

"Righteous," John goes. "I had no idea."

"This is disturbingly hard," Sadie says.

Scott leans over to me and whispers, "That's what she said."

I crack up. Sadie and John look at us.

"What?" John says.

"It's an *Office* thing," I tell him. I smack Scott's arm.

"Ow," he goes.

"As if."

"As *if*," he mocks. I don't know why he's acting so immature instead of acting like part of a couple. I want to jump up on the table, command Bill to shine a spotlight on me, and announce to everyone that Scott and I are together. But I don't think Scott would do any of that.

After the first five rounds, there's an intermission. People line up at the counter for more drinks. A few baristas go around clearing empty mugs and glasses from the tables. One of them reaches for my mug from across the table.

"Beer me that mug," Scott says.

I pass it to him, all giggly. I don't know who this mug-passing giggly girl is. I just know that I love our inside *Office* jokes. It's like we have our own private language or something.

"Is there a reason you guys are keeping all the good jokes to yourselves?" Sadie asks.

I really want to tell them about us. I give Scott a look like, *Can I tell them?* He shrugs, all casual about it.

"Um." I mash my lips together to quit giggling. "We're . . . together now."

"Like . . . *together* together?" Sadie says.

"*Together* together," I confirm.

"When did this happen?" John asks.

"Last night," I say, gazing at Scott. I can feel myself

getting girlier by the second. I still can't believe this is real.

"That's awesome!" Sadie gushes. "You guys are so cute together!"

John stares at me.

"Oh!" Sadie goes. "I almost forgot." She digs around in her massive bag, pulling out some Bliss Body Butter samples. "For you."

"Thanks! I love this stuff." I rub some body butter into my hands.

"Smells nice," Scott observes.

John stares some more.

Things get worse when the next round starts. We were doing pretty well before the break. John knows a lot of random facts. There was a Literary Classics round that I rocked. Not because I'm into literary classics, but because I remember most of that tedium from English classes past. Between Scott and Sadie, we knew a few more answers. But now things are different. No one knows anything about dead presidents. The round after that is Science in the City. John was just telling me about Manhattanhenge the other day, so when Bill asks, "On which two dates will Manhattanhenge take place next year?" I shove the answer form at John, all excited that we finally know something again.

Except John just sits there, staring at his pencil.

"Hello?" I say. "You were just telling me about Manhattanhenge the other day."

"Was I?"

"Come on! I know you know this!"

John gives me a defeated look. "Give it a rest," he says. "We're not in tutoring." He doesn't write anything.

I try to figure it out based on what he told me. Everyone else sips their coffees.

This isn't awkward at all.

"Did you guys arrange the matching before?" Scott asks, pointing at me and Sadie. I have on a shiny silver shirt with a black cardigan and Sadie's wearing a sparkly black shirt with a gray, cropped sweater.

"No," Sadie says. "There's a lot Brooke forgot to tell me before." Her eyes are screaming, *I can't believe you didn't tell me about Scott!* I try to make my eyes say, *Dude, I'll tell you later.* But it's really hard to communicate that in a look.

The next round involves a basket of peppers. Each one is labelled with a number. We have to identify each type of pepper.

"Please tell me one of you knows something about peppers," Sadie begs.

"Sorry," Scott says. "I'm out."

"Number four might be jalapeño," I offer.

John scowls at the peppers.

"Wait." Sadie picks up number seven. "I think this one's cayenne. My mom sometimes tortures us with them when she's in a culinary mood."

We write down our best guesses. John slides the paper in front of him and writes *serrano* for number nine.

When the last round starts, I'm relieved that it's

almost time to go. John has completely shut down. I mean, he probably seems fine to Scott and Sadie, but I know something's wrong. His energy level has dipped. He's actually sitting still.

This one's an audio round, where Bill will play three-second clips of each song. We have to record both the title of the song and the musician. The first two clips are impossible. When the third song comes on Scott and I both go, "I know this one!" Then we're cracking up and yelling for the answer sheet and fighting over a pencil.

It would have been sweet if Two New (we never thought of a better name) bested everyone else. But we didn't. Not even close. Those trivia-night teams are hardcore. It also would have been sweet if I got to spend the rest of the night alone with Scott. But his brother's supposed to call soon and Scott said he really didn't feel like hanging out. I was hoping he'd kiss me before he left. That didn't happen, either. He just gave me a quick hug and took off. John was still in a stank mood when he left. So it's just me and Sadie, walking home together.

"Why didn't you tell me about Scott?!" Sadie yells.

"It was too late to call you last night. I was going to tell you on the way over."

"It's so cool that you guys are together."

"I know."

"How did it happen? Tell me everything."

I tell her everything.

"That," Sadie says, "is intense. You freaking *moved* here for him! How romantic is that?"

"I'm just relieved it worked out."

"You totally belong together. Not that I'm surprised or anything."

"What do you mean?"

"Just that I knew you liked him."

"How?"

"Um, because I've seen you in the same room with him? It's kind of obvious."

This is news. I thought I was being discreet.

"Why didn't you tell me you knew?" I ask.

Sadie takes out a pack of gum. It's that rainbow-stripe kind with the giraffe. "It wasn't any of my business. I figured you'd tell me if you wanted me to know. And after you agreed to be a tutor, I really didn't want to push it."

"After you *harassed* me to be a tutor."

"Did not."

"So did."

Sadie chews her gum. She offers me a piece. I take a green one. "OK, maybe I went after your big brain because I knew you would rule. You have to admit it's fun, right?"

"Hmph."

"Is that a yes?"

"Maybe."

"Oh, you like it!" A biker zips past us at the corner, narrowly missing our noses by about two millimetres.

My heart races at the near-death encounter. Sadie is unfazed. "You're so lucky. I wish Carlos would show up at my door and kiss me."

"Well, maybe he would if he knew you liked him."

"Why should we have to do all the work?"

"Not that Scott *said* he likes me. I mean, I'm assuming he likes me because he kissed me, but then what was with tonight? He didn't even touch me the whole time. And when he left he was all like, 'See ya.' Like I was just a friend or something."

"At least you're friends with him. Carlos doesn't even know I exist." Sadie darts across the street in the middle of the block. I run after her. I'm getting used to her frenzied walking habits, but it's still impossible to predict where she'll zigzag next.

"He knows you exist," I say. "You can't get all flustered the way you do around him without him knowing you exist."

"What if he doesn't, though? What if I ask him out and he's like, '*Have we met?*'"

"You'll never know unless—"

"Or worse! What if he has a girlfriend? I would totally be humiliating myself for nothing."

"It's not nothing."

"It is to him."

"Only because you're not giving him a chance to make it something. If I assumed that nothing would ever happen with Scott, I wouldn't even be here right now. Don't you think I was scared moving here, starting at a new school, not knowing anybody, living with my dad after not even seeing him for six years? We're all scared that people will disappoint us. You think you know someone and then. . ."

"I can't believe you followed Scott here. You took this major risk. You're so much braver than me."

"No I'm not. I just never stopped believing that what I wanted could be real."

This dream came true. The possibility that other dreams could also come true makes me want to turn my life into everything it can be.

NINETEEN

Those couples that celebrate ridiculous things like one-month anniversaries used to irritate me. I mean, really? Does being together for one month really deserve celebration? How is that such a profound accomplishment?

But now that I'm part of a couple, things are different. I don't think celebrating our one-month anniversary is ridiculous at all. Not that I told Scott that's what we're doing today. I was hoping he'd bring it up. When he never did, I decided to keep the celebrating to myself. I'm not sure why I didn't tell him about it. Maybe I was worried he'd think it's stupid.

The middle of November isn't normally the best time for outdoor stuff. But today is freakishly warm. Scott and I have this thing where we explore a new area every week. Today we're doing Union Square. We've been walking around for half an hour and it's already proven itself to be highly explorable territory.

That whole weirdness when Scott wouldn't kiss me or hold my hand is over. All I can think about is making out with him. All I look forward to is the next time we can make out. The parts of my day when I'm not kissing him are unbearable.

"Let's go in here," Scott says.

"Where? The playground?"

"Like you never get an urge to swing."

"All the time. How did you know?"

Scott gently presses me back against the fence. "Because I know you," he says. He presses up against me. Then he kisses me.

A mother passing by with two kids eyes us sharply.

"We should probably wait," I say.

"I hate waiting."

"I know."

At the entrance to the playground, there's a sign that says you can't go in unless you have a child with you. But no one's watching, so we slip in.

"No way!" Scott runs ahead. I follow him. "Talk tubes!"

"Oh, I love these!" I haven't played with talk tubes in for ever. Every time we went on a field trip to the science museum, I'd hog them. How cool is New York for having them in playgrounds?

We take over the talk tubes. I tell Scott how I used to hog them at the science museum. He tells me what he's going to do to me when we get back to his room.

If we could stay in his room permanently, I would have absolutely no problem with that.

Well. Maybe I would. We already spend pretty much all our time in either his room or my room. My room is better because Dad always works late, but I love being in Scott's room. Only, we have to be more creative with our excuses about why we're in there. I'm not sure his mother believes we're spending that much time on homework.

When I used to imagine what it would be like to be Scott's girlfriend, I pictured things a lot differently. We'd have tons in common. We'd never run out of things to talk about. We'd be out all the time, having those exciting city night dates I used to dream about. But things aren't like that. We hardly go anywhere. Sometimes we run out of things to say, which is incredibly awkward. And it doesn't feel like our relationship is moving forward at all. Can I even call it a relationship if it's mostly a physical thing?

I want to tell Scott how I feel. I just don't want him to get mad. The leaving part comes after the getting-mad part.

No one's on the spinning dish. I sit on it while Scott grabs hold and runs to get it going.

"We should go out more," I suggest.

Scott jumps on. "We go out."

"Yeah, but—"

"We went to the movies."

Yeah, one time. It doesn't make sense. Shouldn't two people who love living here as much as we do go out more? I love being alone together, but sometimes it feels like Scott only wants to be with me physically. We don't really have much of an emotional connection. We don't talk about things the way I thought we would. I guess it's because we don't have that much in common. Which people always say is so important, but I don't think it has to be a problem. We have chemistry. Isn't that the most essential part of a relationship? Without chemistry, you're just friends. We definitely have spark. And the making-out part is what I look forward to the most, so why do I even care that we don't do more stuff together? So what if things aren't the way I imagined they would be? When are they ever?

Maybe I should focus on what I have instead of what I don't have. Like how we just got to Scott's place and no one is supposed to be home for two hours.

As soon as he opens the door to his building, we're kissing. I go up the stairs backwards with Scott kissing me the whole time. When we get to his door, Scott digs around in his bag for his keys, still kissing me. I hear the keys hit the floor.

"I might have to stop kissing you to pick those up," Scott whispers, his lips still on mine.

"I'll give you three seconds."

He bends down, grabs his keys, and immediately starts kissing me again.

Scott's room has a powerful effect on me. Just going inside triggers this overwhelming anticipation. Every time I come over, it's like I still can't believe I'm finally here.

I love all the pictures Scott has of his family. He's about four years old in one of them, hugging his dog, Snuffleupagus. That one always makes me want to cry.

There are pictures of Scott white-water rafting and snowboarding. He has a PJ Harvey poster and ticket stubs to a Demetri Martin show. Scott insists Demetri Martin is the funniest comedian in the world. I watched his show at Town Hall online and I agree. He draws these hilarious sketches and plays weird instruments and understands things the way I do. The way *we* do.

We're a *we* now.

As soon as we get to Scott's room, he shuts the door. I lean back against it.

"What's that smile?" Scott says.

"What smile?"

"Like you have a secret or something."

"Oh, it's not a secret. It's totally obvious."

Scott presses up against me and starts kissing me again. I love how he's always pressing up against me. I think it's extremely hot.

"What music do you want to hear?" he asks.

"Whatever you want." Lots of times when we're making out, I don't even notice what's playing. It's like my body can only take so much input, so it blocks out the music to prevent sensory overload.

While Scott goes over to put some music on, I get on his bed. There's something about lying on his bed and looking out the window that feels so familiar. His navy-blue comforter. The heavy curtains on his two windows. The soft glow of the lamp in the corner. It's almost as if I knew what his room would look like before I even got here.

He has a cool view. The building across the street has a penthouse with an enormous patio. A line of electric purple lights runs along the patio's wall. I stare at the purple line, thinking about this new project Mr Peterson assigned. We have to figure out our optimal career path by researching the things we're most passionate about. It's making me realize that the passion I have for New York might be the key to figuring out what I want to do with my life. What if I can channel my love for New York into a career? Like doing something to help make the city a better place and preserve all the things I love the most about it? Preserving what defines the character of this city must be some kind of job. And creating new ways to connect the city environment to the people who live here is probably a real job, too.

"Have you started that new project?" I ask.

"For the Box?"

"Yeah."

"Uh, no. I'm putting it off for as long as possible."

"Why? It sounds fun."

"Fun?" Scott is still searching playlists on his computer. "What's fun about a project that forces us to decide what we want to do?"

"It might work for you. I'm already getting some good ideas."

"I'll pass. There's plenty of time to figure it all out. I really don't need the pressure. I thought you felt the same way."

"I did, but . . . I don't think it's a bad thing to start figuring out what I want to do with my life."

Scott stays focused on the screen. "Whatever," he says.

I can't believe he's not happy for me. He didn't even ask about what I might want to do. I get where Scott's coming from, though. We're like the only two people in our class who don't know where we want to go to college or what we want to do when we get there. We're bonded by indecision. But I'm relieved that I finally have an idea about what I might want to be, even if I don't know exactly what that is yet. Everyone's been spinning around us in this whirlpool of activity while we've been stuck in place together. A couple weeks ago, they all morphed into these academic freakazoids, fretting over application essays and worrying that they might not get into their first-choice college. At some point, I stopped feeling sorry for them and started to envy them.

How can everyone else know exactly where their lives are going? Did they all have an epiphany that Scott and I missed? John has this special social work programme picked out at a college that doesn't give grades. Sadie wants to be an elementary school teacher, which she will rock at. She can get in anywhere she wants.

This could be the answer I've been looking for. Waiting for my real life to start is no excuse to waste the life I have right now. The only reason I'm with Scott is because I took control of my life and changed it to make what I want happen. I created that change myself. Why can't I do the same thing with figuring out my career?

When Scott comes over and gets on top of me, I stop thinking.

Our relationship might not be everything I want. But when we're together like this, everything is perfect. Right here, right now, this is all that matters.

TWENTY

The past two months could not have flown by any faster. The holidays were a blur of turkey and tinsel, divided between here and back home. Mom had Christmas at our house this year, so it was the whole extended family of aunts and uncles and cousins invading our territory. All I could think about was getting back to Scott.

I was hoping that Mom would lay off the criticism since it was a special occasion and all. Not so much. We had variations of the same conversation every day. A typical one went like this:

Mom: Did you finish those college applications?

Me: You asked me that yesterday.

Mom: I'm asking again.

Me: I only have two more with late deadlines.

Mom: What are you waiting for? You're on break; this is when you should be working on them.

Me: [silence]

Mom: April's applying early decision to Worthington University. Did you know that?

Me: Uh, yeah.

Mom: She's going into pre-med. Her mother must
  be so proud.

Me: [silence]

Mom: It must be exciting for her, knowing what she
  wants to do with her life.

And on and on. It was beyond annoying how she
assumed I'm always going to be this directionless loser. I
didn't bother telling her that I've been getting so much
closer to figuring out what I want to do.

It was also annoying how slowly everything
moved back home. I never noticed it before. Everyone
in suburbia is stuck in slow motion, like no one has
anything important they want to accomplish. It's as if no
one is motivated enough by the next thing life has to
offer to want to get there. They even speak slower. The
crazy thing is that none of this used to bother me. But it
grated on my nerves the whole time I was there.

When April called to ask me over, I went. Candice
never showed up. She still didn't want to see me.

"You can't really blame her," April said. Her room
looked different. Her old bookshelf had been replaced
by fitted shelves. Her books were all lined up so you
could see each one. Before they were stacked two or
three deep.

"I didn't think she'd be mad at me for this long," I
said.

April stayed quiet.

Things weren't the same with us. Not at all. I had

been hoping that once we saw each other again things would go back to how they used to be. What's changed other than me moving away? We're still the same people. We should still be best friends. Except we're not. And I don't know if we ever will be again. Especially since April got way harsh with me. She basically accused me of being all snobby with my "new life in the big city", complaining how I bragged about Joe being better than Bean There. I didn't have a whole lot to say after that. I couldn't wait for break to be over.

It's such a relief to be back. Being with Scott again will make all of this irritation go away. At least, I'm hoping it will. We haven't moved forward at all. I was hoping that things would evolve over time. That he would start opening up to me more and we'd connect on a deeper level. Don't boys always take longer to get close in relationships? But what we have still doesn't feel deep enough.

If I were painfully honest with myself, I probably wouldn't even call what we have a relationship. It's more like we have this thing that's never going to be what I want. Unless he's changed over break. Maybe he just needed some time apart to realize how much I mean to him.

Normally, I'm not this kind of girl. It's never taken me hours to fall asleep, lying there with a horrible sinking feeling in my stomach, imagining all the things I'm afraid to say. Keeping everything in is driving me crazy. So I was planning to finally tell Scott everything that's been bothering me right when I saw him again. But I want to give him one more chance. I thought about him the whole time we were apart. I'm sure he thought about me, too.

Finding the perfect Christmas present for Scott was my main goal over break. We were going to exchange gifts before I left, but Scott said he wouldn't have a chance to get me anything. Maybe he just said that so I'd be surprised by how awesome my gift is. He's probably known exactly what he wants to get me all along.

When the doorbell rings, I race out of my room to buzz Scott up. My heart pounds as I hear him getting closer. I fling the door open before he can knock. And there he is. Smiling and holding out my present.

"I missed you," I say.

"I missed you, too."

And then we're kissing and moving into my room and I forget about our presents for the next few hours. All of the bad feelings I've had about us evaporate.

Eventually, Scott says, "I'm starving."

"Do you want to order in?"

"Totally. It's so cool your dad lets you do that."

"Like he has a choice. You know he's never home for dinner. And I don't cook."

I pull Scott off my bed and lead him to the kitchen. My present was abandoned by the door when he got here. I'd put it under the tree if our tree were big enough to put presents under. This tree is embarrassing. It's this little fake one Dad bought a few days before

Christmas. He's never here for Christmas because he always goes to my uncle's house in Massachusetts, so this is the first time he's had his own tree. The tree sits on an end table, looking sad. And silver. I get that a big tree like we always have back home wouldn't work in this apartment, but couldn't he have at least got a green tree? Even if it's fake? Dad seems to like it, though. And I got to pick out the ornaments, so it's not completely heinous.

While Scott goes through the take-out menus, I take my present over to the couch for inspection. I can tell he wrapped it himself. The ends are all crooked and he used too much tape. It just makes me love him more.

"How about pizza?" Scott asks.

"Pizza's good."

"What do you want on it?"

"Whatever you want." I'm trying to guess what my present is from the size of the box, which I would classify as medium small. Too big to be jewellery. Too small to be a bag. Not the right shape for a book or DVD. It could be—

"What do think you're doing?" Scott says, suddenly behind me.

"Nothing." I gaze up at him with wide eyes, all innocent. "I was just looking. Not opening."

"You sure about that?"

"Positive. See?" I hold my present up.

"Hmm. Well, the pizza is ordered. The presents are in the house. I think it's time."

"Yay!" I run to my room, grab Scott's present, and leap back onto the couch. "It's like Christmas all over again! Except this time it doesn't suck!"

"Sorry going home was such a drag. Every time you called, I wished I could come out there and rescue you."

"No worries. It's over. Anyway, New York is my home now."

"You really think you'll be here next year?"

"Yeah. I mean, I hope so." Why did he say "*you'll be here next year*" instead of "*we'll be here next year*"? I thought we were planning to go to the same college, or at least ones close to each other. That's why we both applied to some of the same colleges in Manhattan.

I squash the bad feelings down.

"Who's going first?" I ask. I don't know what I'm more excited about – Scott opening his present or me opening mine.

"You can go."

"No, you go."

"Are you sure?"

"Uh-huh!" I yell, bouncing on the couch like I'm three years old. I cannot *wait* for him to see how perfect his present is.

Scott rips off the wrapping paper. I was kind of hoping he'd say something about it. I spent half an hour picking out the exact right paper and bow. Did he even see the bow? The bow was a masterpiece.

"Oh, wow," he says. After endless deliberation over the perfect gift, I decided to get him a Dunder Mifflin mouse pad and World's Best Boss mug. It's funny because at first I was going to get him *Office* stuff. Then I was worried it wouldn't be a surprise, so I spent hours going to stores with my cousins over break, searching for the perfect unexpected gift. A gift so perfect that he'd never see it coming, never even realize it's what he wanted. But in the end, I trusted my initial instinct. I wanted him to have things he could use every day that he'd love.

Scott laughs at the mug. "Hilarious." He picks up the mouse pad. "I already have a mouse pad, though."

"I know. But that one's so old and I knew you'd love this one."

"Thanks."

"You love it, right?"

"As much as a person can love a mouse pad."

Eff. I knew I should have got something more personal. I'm such an idiot.

I squash the bad feelings down some more.

"Your turn," he says.

When I unwrap my present, I just sit there. This must be some kind of mistake.

I'm like, "Cayenne pepper–flavoured chocolate?"

"I know! Can you believe they even make that?"

"Um. No. I really can't."

"Try some."

Who is this boy and what did he do with Scott Abrams? Does he seriously believe I would like something as hideous as cayenne pepper–flavoured chocolate? When has he ever seen me eat anything even remotely that disgusting?

Then it hits me. This must be a joke. This is a joke and he's hiding my real present somewhere else.

"Ha ha," I go. "Give it."

"What?"

"You know what."

"I don't think I do."

Scott is serious. Scott seriously gave me this as my Christmas present. I spent hours agonizing over the perfect gift for him, and what does he do? He gives me something I would never eat in a million years.

Does he even know who I am?

The stomach churning that's been keeping me awake every night hits me full force. I hold my hand against my stomach, willing those bad feelings to stay down.

I take out the chocolate and read the label. "Exotic. Where did you find this kind of . . . chocolate?"

"At the mall yesterday," Scott says, looking pleased with himself.

He went to the mall yesterday to get my present? *Yesterday?* He had the whole freaking break and he went – you know what, it doesn't even matter. It's just a stupid gift. Since when are material things so important? Why am I acting like such a princess?

Maybe because there's no way someone who gets me the way I want to be got would give me something so clueless.

This isn't about some nasty chocolate. It's about the truth that I keep trying to squash down, that keeps bubbling back up to the surface. I already know how the rest of the night's going to go. We'll watch TV while we eat pizza. We won't look at each other or talk to each other. Then we might make out some more if my dad still isn't home yet. If he is, Scott will leave. He won't stay here just to be with me. We won't talk about anything that matters. Scott used to talk about his brother or vent about college essays. It felt like he was opening up to me more, letting me into his life in a real way. I can't remember the last time he talked about anything serious.

But it's not like we're going to break up. I didn't move all the way here for things to not work out. I've loved Scott for so long. We just can't go on like this.

Even as I'm trying to figure out how to make this right, an irritating question won't leave me alone. If things were going to change, wouldn't they have changed by now?

TWENTY-ONE

I've thought about it. A lot.

Conclusion: the only way to know if things will ever change is to ask Scott how he feels about me.

When school started again yesterday, I avoided him outside of class. But it was awesome catching up with Sadie. I didn't realize how much I missed her until she was right there again.

If things don't change with Scott, my stomach churning will only get worse. I want to be happier. I want us to be the kind of couple I know we can be. So I'm the one who has to make that change happen.

When Scott gets to Crumbs, I wave to him confidently. Everything will be OK. It has to be. I even managed to save a table for us despite several attempts by mothers to swipe Scott's chair.

Scott kisses me. Even after all the times he's kissed me, I still get a total rush. I don't think I'll ever get used to him kissing me, no matter how long we're together. To me it will always be like, *No* way! *Scott Abrams is kissing me!*

"What's that one?" Scott asks about my cupcake.

He thinks it's cute how Sadie has got me hooked on Crumbs. I wasn't particularly into cupcakes before. I mean, of course I liked them. Who doesn't like cupcakes? I just never obsessed about flavours and frosting and sprinkles the way this whole subculture of cupcake fanatics does. Sadie belongs to that group. Her obsession has apparently influenced me because now I'm a Crumbs fan.

"It's the Cupcake of the Week," I say.

"What kind is it?"

"Piña Colada. I love the little umbrella. It's golden cake with lemon pineapple filling and coconut frosting. With a cherry on top, as you can see."

"I can't believe you haven't eaten the cherry yet."

"I wanted you to see all the parts."

After Scott gets a cupcake (the Squiggle one, which tastes exactly like a chocolate Hostess Cup Cake – they even put the swirly line of vanilla icing on top) and coffee, it's time to be free of everything that's been bothering me.

"Not to get all heavy?" I say. "But I need to talk to you about something."

"Shoot."

"Um . . . well, I was just . . . wondering where things are going."

"What things?"

"Things with us."

"Like . . . how do you mean?"

How can Scott not know what I mean? Isn't asking

where things are going the universal code for wanting the other person to define the relationship?

"It seems like . . . OK, you know I love being with you. I'm just wondering how you feel about us. Because to me, it feels like things aren't moving to the next level and I don't know why."

Scott glances at a little boy at the next table. His mom is watching him eat a mint chocolate chip cupcake. The boy has green frosting on his cheek.

"Are we talking about sex?" Scott says quietly.

"No. I mean the next emotional level. Like opening up to each other more."

"I told you about Ross, didn't I?"

"Yeah, but we haven't really talked about anything else that matters. It seems like things are kind of . . . superficial. I just think we should be more serious by now. But it feels like you're afraid to get closer or something."

"Me?"

"Sort of."

"That's ironic."

"Meaning?"

"You're the one who doesn't let people in."

"That's not true." I thought I was doing better here. I thought New Me was making friends. What about Sadie? She's practically my best friend now. And what about John? Old Me never would have been friends with him.

Scott leans back in his chair, rubbing his hands over

his face. A group of middle school girls comes crashing in, all loud shrieks and general ruckus.

"Why are you doing this?" he says.

"I'm just telling you how I feel. Shouldn't people in a relationship be able to tell each other how they feel?"

"Yeah, but why do we have to get so serious? I like the way things are. I thought you did, too."

"I do . . . mostly. It just feels like we're standing still."

"We haven't been together that long."

"It's long enough to know if we want more."

Scott's looking at me like I'm crazy for saying all this. I can understand where he's coming from. To him, we've been together for less than three months. But to me, we've been connected for so much longer. Everything I want us to be has been building up for more than two years. It's like a part of me has belonged to him the whole time. And yeah, maybe I'm acting crazy, but this whole thing was crazy. It was crazy to leave my entire life behind to follow some boy here. It's crazy that I'm unhappy when I should be ecstatic. To Scott, it's crazy that I want a major commitment so soon. But it doesn't feel soon to me. It feels like I've been waiting to have something real with him for ever.

"We've been having fun," Scott says. "Isn't that what senior year's about? We – hanging out with you is cool. Why can't that be enough?"

Hanging out? Is that what he thinks we've been doing this whole time? He makes it sound so casual.

"Because it's not," I say. "Because I moved here to

be with you. I wouldn't have dropped everything and changed my entire life for someone I wasn't serious about."

The shrieky group of girls descends on the table next to us. It would have been better if Scott came over to my place. I don't know why I asked him to meet me here.

"You don't think that puts pressure on me?" Scott says. "What am I supposed to do with that? How am I supposed to live up to this person you want me to be?"

"You're—"

"I don't think I can be the person you want. I really . . . I don't think I'm enough for you."

"But you are! I know you better than you think."

"Do you? You watched me for two years and then followed me here. How is that knowing someone?"

When we started going out and I told Scott how I felt about him, how I knew him without having to be someone he knew back, I thought he understood. I thought he got me. But I'm realizing that he doesn't get me at all.

"You mean so much to me," I say. "I thought you knew that."

"I do. That's why it's impossible to live up to your expectations. This is who I am. I can't be someone I'm not."

Shrieky Girls are squealing over how good the Cupcake of the Week is. Green Frosting Boy is throwing a tantrum. He wants to finish his cupcake, but his mother is taking half of it home. Meanwhile, my own personal tragedy is playing out here at the Table of Rejection. I am Breakdown amidst the sugar high. I've never felt so alone in a crowd.

Shrieky Girls are looking at me.

Leaning over the table, I whisper, "I'm sorry you feel pressured." There's no stopping the tears. I angrily wipe my eyes.

"Don't cry," Scott says. He slides his napkin over to me. "Didn't you say you've always wanted to live here? Way before I was even in the picture?"

I nod.

"So now you're here! That's a good thing, right?"

Not without you. The dream of you and the dream of living here were intertwined. Those dreams go together the way you and I were supposed to.

I wipe my nose. I avoid eye contact with Green Frosting Boy's mom.

Scott goes, "Can't we just . . . keep it fun?"

It's so tempting to say yes, to be with him however he wants me to be. But I've been playing this whole time. I desperately want to be that girl who can have fun city nights with a boy she loves and not want anything more. Ever since Scott kissed me, I've been trying to be that girl. I'm just not her. If Scott and I can't be together the way I know we should be in my heart, then I can't do this any more.

"No," I say. "That would be a lie."

"What are you saying?"

"That . . . I can't do this. I can't have only part of you. That's not why I came here."

"Can we still be friends?"

"I don't know. I have to think about it."

Scott scoots his chair back and gets up. "Then I'll give you some room to do that," he says.

And just like that, I'm back to being all alone.

TWENTY-TWO

Welcome to the Worst Day Ever.

"Don't be friends with him," Sadie advises. "That would be a world of pain."

"I can't believe I moved here for him," I say. "What was I thinking?"

How can this be the end? It was just the beginning.

When Sadie got to my place after school, I couldn't tell her what happened with Scott right away. I couldn't talk to her the whole day. I couldn't talk to anyone. It felt like I was on the verge of crying every second. Despite desperately trying to remain calm, I had to run to the bathroom twice when tears suddenly started pouring down my face. I cut my last two classes and came home early. There's no way I was sitting next to Scott the day after he broke my heart.

Nothing is going to be OK. Nothing is ever OK.

Sadie sinks lower into my beanbag chair, quiet for the first time since I asked her to come over. This day could not get any worse. It's all cold and dreary out. A slogging, depressing wintry mix has been falling on and off. Oh yeah, and Scott doesn't want to be my boyfriend any more unless we keep things casual.

I press a wet tissue against my eyes.

"He wasn't the right boy for you," Sadie says. "The right boy would never make you feel this way."

"But I really believed he was."

"Relationships should move forward naturally. Both people should want that. If there's resistance, you know there's a problem."

"Oh, there's a problem."

"Not any more. Now you can find a boy who would do anything to be with you."

"I don't want to be with anyone."

"No, I know you don't now. But you will one day. And when you're ready, you'll know what to look for."

I pull a fresh tissue out of the box. It's nice of Sadie to try to make me feel better. Being with someone new is the last thing I want to think about, but I know that everything she's saying is right.

"So ... how's John doing in tutoring? Are you seeing any improvement?"

"Some." Things with John aren't exactly the same any more. I mean, we still talk about the same stuff and he still jokes around with me, but we haven't gone to the High Line in for ever. It's too cold to stay out for more than a few minutes. It feels like being locked up in school has also locked part of him away from me.

"As if I could think about anything other than Scott right now," I say.

"At least you have boy confidence," Sadie notes. "At least you put yourself out there."

"Yeah. Look how well that worked out."

"But look at what you did. You were a freaking couple! You made it happen!"

Sadie grabs her massive bag and rummages around in it until she finds a notebook. She throws the cover open. She rummages around some more, eventually producing her trademark glittery purple pen. Then she starts scribbling frantically.

"What are you—"

"Sshhh!" Sadie keeps scribbling, holding up a finger to get me to wait. A few minutes later, she yanks the page out of her notebook. "Can you fold this into any animal?"

"Pretty much."

"Can you do a lizard?"

"Probably. Do I get to read it first?"

"No."

"Or know who it's for?"

"I'll tell you after."

I do my best to fold Sadie's note into a lizard. His tail comes out sort of scrunched.

"Awesome," Sadie declares. "Let's go."

Walking around in the gross wintry mix is the last thing I want to do, but Sadie insists. I grudgingly pull on my boots and everything else. My hat is still wet from before.

When we're on our way to somewhere she still

won't tell me, she says, "So here's what I'm thinking. Boy confidence can only be gained by intense practice sessions. You've had boy confidence for a really long time. Not that moving here wasn't hard for you, it was just easier since you were used to boys treating you a certain way."

"They didn't—"

Sadie gives me the hand. "You changed your whole life to be with Scott. The least I could do is try to be with Carlos."

"Finally!" I look around for Scott. I'm paranoid that I'll see him.

"He's working today, so. . ."

"What does the note say?"

"I went for the less-is-more strategy. It basically just has my number."

"Are you aware that you rule?"

"I will rule when he calls me. Until then, I am still lame."

When we get to Rite Aid, I wait outside. It's a weird feeling, being happy for your friend's boy situation but depressed about your own at the same time.

A few minutes later, Sadie comes out. She's not happy the way I expected her to be. She's more like devastated. And she still has the note.

"What happened?" I say.

"I couldn't give it to him."

"Oh. Well, we'll come back another day. You can try again."

"No. I couldn't give it to him because he doesn't work here any more."

"Why not?"

"I don't know. All the manager said was that Carlos gave notice two weeks ago. He doesn't know where he went."

"We can still find him. Do you know his last name?"

"No."

"We can ask the manager."

"What, so I can be known as the loser who hunts down random Rite Aid cashiers? I don't think so."

"But—"

"You know what we need?"

"What?"

"Cupcakes."

So we go to Crumbs. Sometimes in the midst of all your boy drama, you just need a cupcake.

One thing I love about New York is how quickly your life can change. Take right now, for example. I'm suddenly on my way to NYU. While I was waiting for Sadie to pick which cupcake she wanted at Crumbs (she went with the Good Guy), I was looking at their big bulletin board where you can post flyers about local events and stuff. There was a flyer for this urban-planning-project presentation at NYU. Which saved me, because otherwise I would have gone home and cried about Scott all night.

When I was doing research for that career project

we had for the Box, I found out about urban planning. It's the exact field I was thinking about, except I didn't know it was called urban planning. Urban planners create green spaces like the High Line, or develop ways to make built structures more appealing to city residents, or focus on ways to incorporate more natural light and green energy into renovated buildings. If I decide to become an urban planner, I can major in environmental studies or sociology as an undergrad, then get a master's degree in urban planning. So when I saw the flyer, I knew I had to go.

I've seen college brochures featuring pictures of sprawling campuses with lots of grass and massive, scholarly looking buildings all spread out. NYU isn't like that. There's not enough space here for it to have an actual campus. Even though it's basically just some buildings bunched together over a few blocks, I can still feel the energy of college life. Students are swishing past me in all directions, some underdressed in bulky sweatshirts and thick scarves, others sealed up tight in puffy coats. I imagine what it must feel like to be on your own, throwing on a sweatshirt in your dorm room and running to class at the last minute, all excited for a first date you have with that cute boy from economics later. Everyone rushes past me while I try to find the right building. It's a relief when I finally find it because I'm freezing.

As soon as I get to the conference room, this jolt of inspiration hits me. For the first time ever, I can totally see myself at a place like this, working towards a life that won't only make me happy but will make other people happy as well.

I've never been to a grad student–project presentation before, or any college event. It's way more crowded than I expected. And kind of upscale. Even though this is a really old building, the conference room is all renovated, with shiny hardwood floors and big, new windows. You can see Washington Square Park with its illuminated arch. There's even a coat check that I almost walk right by until a girl calls after me, "Would you like to check your coat?" I just smile and take my coat off and try not to look as intimidated as I feel.

There are rows of long tables with students standing behind their areas. The room is filled with people weaving around the rows. People who belong here. I am so out of place I don't even know which way to go.

Other people appear to be going right up to the presenters and asking them about their projects. Trying to blend in, I slowly walk along the first row of tables. Each student's area has a big, foam-core poster board bent in three sections with their project description. Some of them also have laptops showing videos. And there are all kinds of materials, like glass samples and building models and even a wind turbine.

I stop to read a poster board about the built environment. There's a synopsis of a study about how increased personal investment in urban living spaces decreases poverty levels. Then there's a project on

MillionTreesNYC, which is this initiative to plant one million new trees throughout the city. The idea is to encourage neighbourhood revitalization, help reduce pollutants, and introduce a cooling factor to the urban heat island effect. These projects are incredible. There are so many ways I could share my passion for this city by becoming an urban planner. I can almost feel the synapses firing in my brain, processing ideas.

One girl has a huge picture of the High Line on her poster board. I go up to her.

"The High Line rules," I say.

"I know, isn't it phenomenal?"

"Beyond phenomenal. What's your project about?"

"Green building design. I'm interested in how green spaces and green architecture improve the well-being of urban residents."

"That's exactly what I'm interested in!"

"Would you like to hear about what I'm doing?"

I nod enthusiastically. As she explains the parts of her project, I'm blown away. The more she explains, the more intense this calming sensation of clarity becomes.

Suddenly, The Knowing comes in. And I know without a shadow of a doubt that this is what I'm meant to do.

TWENTY-THREE

Something's wrong with John.

It's been hard enough trying to function normally since the breakup. Trying to put my issues aside so I can help John with this time zones worksheet is even harder. But trying to help John when he's being so hostile? Is practically impossible.

"Are you sure nothing's wrong?" I ask. I've already asked John what's wrong and he's already told me nothing. I don't believe him. He's totally low energy today. And he's been giving off these angry vibes ever since I sat down at our usual table.

"Can we just do this?" John goes. "What's that thing about the International Date Line again?"

"Why are you mad at me?"

John clicks his pen on and off a bunch of times. Then he drops it on the worksheet. "Does December twenty-third mean anything to you?"

"Um . . . not really."

"No? Let me refresh your memory. We were supposed to meet at the Film Forum to see *Office Space*. Ring a bell now?"

"Oh my god, I'm so sorry! I completely forgot!"

"Ya think?"

"I was really looking forward to it."

"Could have fooled me."

"Scott called a few hours before about this thing that happened with his brother and I had to go over and—"

"You could have at least called."

"I know! I was going to and then. . ." I don't know what to say to John. I totally forgot to call him that night before the movie started. I kept meaning to call him and apologize over break, but it just slipped away.

"Whatever," John goes. "Let's just get this over with."

"Please don't be mad. It was stupid of me not to call. I'm really sorry."

I'm so mad at myself for hurting John. I owe him a lot. My urban-planning epiphany at NYU last night was initially inspired by him. He was the first one to show me that other people feel the same energy I do just by being here. I talked to lots of students last night, and seeing how passionate they were made me realize that John and I aren't alone.

Those days on the High Line with John pointing out all these amazing details I might never have noticed . . . I didn't realize it at the time, but he woke me up. He made me care about where my life is going.

"I knew it had to do with Scott," John grumbles.

"What did?"

"You know what?" John yanks his bag up on the table, jamming his stuff in. "I'm done."

"But I thought you wanted to go over the International Date Line again."

"I'll figure it out."

Watching him leave, I'm not relieved to get out of tutoring the way I would have been before. Tutoring him has done more for me than I expected. I didn't expect to be inspired. I didn't expect to wake up. And I definitely didn't expect to figure out what my future would look like. John helped me understand who I am and he doesn't even know it.

Every time the phone rings, my heart races.

I keep hoping Scott will call.

He keeps not calling.

Here's one for the Of Course file. While I'm in the bathroom, the doorbell rings. I have no idea who it is. Whoever it is only rings once.

I'm sure it was Scott. He was walking by and realized he doesn't want to lose me. He's desperate to get me back. And I missed sharing this revelation because I was in the freaking bathroom.

Eff.

OK, think. If it was Scott, where would he be going? There's a possibility he came over to see if I was home and then went back to his place. But if he wasn't being spontaneous about ringing my bell, wouldn't he have called first?

The sandwich shop is closer to my place than his. I bet he's on his way there. Maybe I'll just swing by to see if Scott's there. If he's there and he looks happy to see me, then I'll know for sure it was him.

Skulking by the sandwich shop, I casually glance in.

Scott is at his usual table.

With Leslie.

Dad just got home, which is shocking. He never gets home before seven. I used to believe him when he said he'd be home for dinner. I believed him when he said we'd go running along the river every Sunday, or that we'd do something touristy some weekend. It didn't take long to realize that Dad's never home for dinner. We only went running like three times and then he totally forgot about it. We don't spend time together at all. The few times Dad has eaten dinner with me, he was talking on the phone or watching the news. He's never going to change his habits, no matter how many times he promises that tomorrow will be different. Because when tomorrow comes, he'll still be the same person he was the day before. Just another guy who's let me down.

I am extraneous. I am nonessential. I'm just someone taking up space in the guest room.

I should have never come here. Did I really think that everything would turn out the way I hoped it would? Life doesn't work that way.

People always let you down. Even the ones you trust.

Especially the ones you trust.

"Brooke?" Dad yells from the kitchen. "You here? I got Chinese."

The air fills with his coming-home sounds. Keys clanking against the table. Takeaway bags landing on the counter. The TV turning on. All the same sounds that he would make even if no one else was here to listen.

My father's daughter moved in with him and he hasn't changed his life at all.

I go out to the living room. Dad's on the couch, already clicking away on his laptop.

"Hey there, kiddo," he says. "Dinner's in the kitchen."

"Since when?"

Dad looks up from his laptop. "Since . . . I brought home Chinese?"

"How could you do that to us?"

"I thought you liked Chinese."

"How could you walk out on your family? What kind of father leaves his kid like that?"

It's obvious that Dad wasn't expecting this. I wasn't expecting to say these things, either, but there you go. The past doesn't just disappear after it's happened. The rage I've been trying to ignore can't be ignored any longer.

"I wanted to stay in your life," Dad says. "You know that."

"You're not even with that other woman any more. Was it more important to be with some random woman for like two seconds than to stay with your family?"

"It might have looked that way, but I can assure you that wasn't the case. Staying with your mother would have been the worst decision for all of us."

"At least Mom was easier to get along with when you were there. Do you know how hard it is to talk to her now? All she ever does is tear me apart for not doing better in school. All these years of fighting with her are your fault."

"Brooke." Dad looks at the wall, as if what he should say next will be written there. "Your mother became impossible to live with. Would you rather I stayed so you could see us fighting all the time? That would have been worse for you."

"There were other ways to stay in my life."

"Which you didn't want any part of!" Dad yells. "You never returned my calls. You didn't visit when I invited you. Can you blame me for eventually giving up?"

"You didn't want me!" I yell back. "You were just doing those things so you could feel better about yourself for leaving."

"That's not—"

"What would we have done if I called you back? Talk on the phone every few weeks? Maybe I'd visit you once a year? What kind of family is that?"

"I didn't know you were still angry about this."

"Of course I am. Why wouldn't I be? And that thing with Justine? What *was* that?"

Dad's eyes get huge. "What thing?"

"I saw you, OK? I know you guys were. . ." There's no way I can say that I saw them kissing. It's just too disgusting.

"I don't know what you think you saw, but nothing happened with Justine."

"Why are you lying? I said I *know*." I feel all shaky and gross. I hate this.

Dad rubs his hands over his face. He knows he can't deny it.

"Why am I even here?" I say.

"You asked if you could stay with me."

"That's the only reason? Because I asked?"

"Of course not. You know I invited you several times. You're always welcome here."

"What's the point? You're never home."

Dad starts to say something else, but I'm not interested. I go to my room and collapse on my bed, exactly where I collapsed after I got back from the Scott and Leslie sandwich shop debacle.

I have a new wish for my wish box. Just once, I wish I could know what it feels like to trust someone completely and not have them disappoint you.

TWENTY-FOUR

After the fight with my dad, I had to get out of there. I quickly threw a change of clothes and some essentials in my bag. There was no way I'd go back tonight or before school tomorrow. Then I called Sadie. When her mom told me she wasn't home, I decided to walk around until she got back. Dad didn't even try to stop me when I left.

I want to run away into the night and never come back. Take a train to anywhere. Find a better life.

My rage burns. I could totally walk all the way back to New Jersey. I could walk around all night. I hardly even feel how cold it is with this fire blazing inside me. I stomp from pavement to pavement, not looking around the way I usually do. I don't look up. Looking up is for people who still have hope.

When I'm walking at night, I'm usually all about the city lights and buzzing energy and excitement over everything around me, the repeated realization that I'm part of it all. But tonight, staring down at the pavements, I'm noticing how dirty they are. And how everyone's rubbish bags are piled up on the kerbs instead of in rubbish bins. A huge rat is rummaging through one of the rubbish piles like he owns the place. It's not like I didn't know that scuzzy parts of the city existed. I've just never really noticed them before.

I pass a homeless guy digging through a rubbish bin on the corner. Suddenly, being here isn't so exciting any more. This place is depressing. People sleep on the streets because they have nowhere to go. It's like we're living in some inhumane world where no one cares about anyone else. People break into apartments or mug people right on the street. Girls get raped, or even killed. Anything could happen to me out here.

The homeless guy is watching me. We're the only ones around. This is one of the gorgeous, quiet streets I love. But tonight things are different. There's nothing to love about being eyeballed by some sketchy dude rooting through the rubbish.

It's time to go.

I call Sadie on her mobile, but it goes straight to voice mail. Her mom said she's at a random-acts-of-kindness event and might not get home until late. I can't wait that long. So I make a snap decision about where to go. It might be the worst decision I've ever made, but I know it's somewhere safe.

The High Line looks spectacular at night. The trees are all illuminated. Everything always seems so peaceful here, like no matter how horrible life gets you can always count on this.

John's mom answers the door. I met her one time when we were out here for tutoring. A crazy downpour suddenly started and we made a run for John's place. It was so comforting inside. John's sister Hailey immediately asked me a million questions even though we'd just met. We all ate warm chocolate chip cookies and watched the rain.

"Hi, Mrs Dalton," I say. "Is John here?"

"He should be back in a minute. I sent him to the store for milk." Mrs Dalton steps aside. "Come in, come in, get out of the cold."

"Thanks." I'm relieved to be in their warm living room. That comforting sensation from the last time I was here is right here again.

Hailey comes out of her room to see who it is.

"Hey, Brooke!" she squeals. "I haven't seen you in for ever. What did you get for Christmas? I got this awesome bracelet I wanted and two Cranium games – Wow and Hullabaloo – and this art set that real artists use. Look at our tree! Want to see the ornaments I made?"

"OK, why don't we let Brooke take her coat off?" Mrs Dalton says. "Would you like a hot chocolate?"

"That would be perfect," I tell her.

"Hailey, please put out another mug for Brooke."

Hailey runs off to the kitchen.

"Sorry she's a bit hyper. Hailey's dad sent her a huge tin of maple sugar. I was rationing it out, but she found my hiding place earlier."

"That's OK. I get hyper, too, sometimes."

Mrs Dalton laughs. "I'll hang up your coat – want to put your scarf with it?"

"Thanks."

"As soon as John gets back with the milk, I'll put the hot chocolate on. Hailey should be OK about not having any. I've already explained to her that she's reached her sugar limit for the week." Mrs Dalton takes my coat. Then she says, "I want to thank you for everything you've done for John. It's really made a difference. He seems to be understanding things in a new way that's working for him."

"That's awesome. I'm glad I can help."

"You definitely are. Whatever you're doing, please keep up the good work."

Mrs Dalton is one of those super informed moms. John told me all about her. She's a child psychologist who has all these connections within the school system. In a way, John's lucky. Because his mom has money and knows the right people, he gets the services he needs. Like how he has a private tutor on top of the help he gets at school. If Mrs Dalton wasn't so dedicated to John's success, he probably wouldn't be so amazing.

Hailey races back out to the living room. Actually, I think it's called a great room. It's just one big space with enormous windows along the wall, looking out over the High Line.

"Come see my ornaments!" Hailey yells, pulling on my arm.

The first ornament that catches my eye is a delicate, clear dove with white feathers and glitter.

"I love this one," I say.

"I didn't make that one. I made this one." Hailey shows me a star. "And this one." An angel. "And . . . wait, where did it go? Oh, here it is – this one."

"They're pretty."

"So are you. Did you know that John likes you?"

"What?"

"I'm back!" John yells, closing the door behind him. His coat is half off and he's unwrapping his scarf when he sees us by the tree.

"Sorry I didn't call or anything," I say. "I really needed to come over."

John unwraps the rest of his scarf. He takes his coat off. He's wearing a thermal with a T-shirt over it. His shirt has the outline of a water tower and says LOOK UP.

"Is it OK that I'm here?" I ask.

"Yeah. Just let me give this to my mom."

We watch John take the deli bag to the kitchen. Then I whisper to Hailey, "He likes me?"

"He *totally* likes you," she whispers fiercely. "You're like all he talks about."

"Since when?"

"Since you met."

"Why didn't—"

"So what's up?" John says.

It takes me a second to get my thoughts together. Is Hailey right? Does John like me? I never saw our relationship that way at all. I was just happy that I could actually be friends with a boy who didn't have some ulterior motive. It was easy to tell if boys liked me back home. Some of them ran game, but they were always transparent.

"Can I talk to you?" I say.

"Let's go to my room."

Hailey is struck by a fit of snorting laughter.

"Don't snort out a tonsil or anything," John advises.

"Ew! Why do you have to be so gross?"

"I'm a boy. We're all gross."

Last time I was here, I didn't really see John's room. He has one of those rooms where you know exactly who it belongs to. Flyers from trivia nights at The Situation Room are taped over his dresser, where two Rubik's Cubes are sitting. His closet door is flung open. Clothes are scattered everywhere. I recognize a bunch of his hoodies, some hanging up, some on the floor. There's a black poster of a burnt, red stapler with smoke coming out of it. Along the bottom in yellow it says, I BELIEVE YOU HAVE MY STAPLER.

The thing I'm most impressed with is a huge photo of New York City at night taken over our neighbourhood. It has glittery gold streets leading downtown, midnight purple water surrounding the edge of Manhattan, and New Jersey lights shining in the distance. The Twin Towers stand proudly over everything.

"I love this poster," I say.

"Thanks. I knew you would."

"I had a really bad fight with my dad. I can't go back there. I know you're mad at me, but do you think I could stay here tonight?"

"You know you can."

"Sweet, *thank* you."

"That's part of the problem. You know I can't say no to you."

"Um . . . I wasn't sure if it would be OK. I could go if—"

"But what pisses me off the most? Isn't even about me. It's about how you can disrespect yourself and not even care. You have this amazing gift that you're just throwing away. I wish I had even one shred of your talent. Stuff that takes me hours to figure out comes so easily to you, like it's nothing. Don't you realize how lucky you are? It's like . . . why are you doing this to yourself? You could be so much more than you let yourself be. You *are* so much more. Why can't you just let yourself be the real you?"

I'm completely blown away. I have no idea what to say to all that. Hailey must have been right about John liking me. Why else would he care so much?

"I didn't know that's why you were mad," I say. "Why didn't you say anything before?"

"I'm not mad. I'm disappointed. There's a difference."

"Can—"

"No, wait. I *am* mad. I'm mad that from the second I saw you, I knew I wanted to be with you, but you didn't feel the same way. It really felt like you came here for me, but you actually came here for Scott. Then suddenly, it's all about him and I'm like, *Where did* this *guy come from?* I couldn't believe you asked him to go to Strawberry Fields with us."

"Wait. Sadie and I were supposed to go alone, but then you said you wanted to come. It's not like it was originally the three of us."

"Dude. I'm the one who asked Sadie to set the whole thing up. I asked her to ask you to go. And the next thing I know, you're hanging all over Scott right in front of me. I couldn't stand it. I even had to get off the subway early. And that time on the roof when I tried to hold your hand? You didn't even notice. That's . . . I really thought we were connecting. Then I find out you liked Scott the whole time."

"Wow."

"Tell me about it."

"This is. . ." How could I have been so clueless? John is the first boy I've ever misread. I wasn't even sure if he liked girls. He never talked about any. And I never asked because I assumed it was part of his life he wanted to keep private. This is not at all what I expected.

John coughs. "I sort of wish I could take back everything I just said."

"It's OK. I'm glad you told me."

"Really? Won't things be weird now?"

"I don't think so."

There's no way I want John out of my life just because he likes me. As long as it's not weird for him, I'm cool with it. Actually, I'm extremely thankful that John is in my life. He's such a good friend. It's obvious that he wants me to be the best version of myself. He's helped me realize my potential in a way my mom never could and my dad is never around to encourage. While Mom shoots me down and keeps saying how much of a disappointment I am, John picks me up. He helped me figure out what I want to be. He motivates me to care. He's helping me way more than I'm helping him. He always makes me feel better, even if all we're doing is discovering new water towers or walking around, looking up.

So how incredible is it that John was able to do all of those things without telling me how he felt? It must have been really hard for him to put my needs before his own. And that makes him even more amazing than I realized.

"It's funny how you wore that shirt tonight," I say. It's like John somehow knew I'd need to come over. I can't remember what he was wearing in tutoring before, but it wasn't this. This, I would have remembered. "It's new, right?"

"Yeah. I had it customized at that place on MacDougal."

"Is being friends going to be weird for you?"

"Probably. But I'd rather get used to it than lose you. Want to know what my autumnal equinox resolution was?"

"OK."

"To find a way to make you realize that we belong together."

Shut. Up. I am totally sticking that in the Of Course file. Because of course that's the same resolution I made about Scott. I remember that day on the High Line, seeing it for the first time, overwhelmed not only by the beauty of it but by John connecting with this city the same way I do. I remember the sunset we watched. And I remember how relaxed I felt with him.

John could not be further from relaxed right now. He's a total wreck. He's been pacing around his room, picking random stuff up and throwing it back down.

I feel horrible. "I'm really sorry about this," I apologize.

"Don't be. You either feel it or you don't."

"I love spending time with you. I don't want that to change."

"No change necessary. Let the record show that life will resume as usual."

"Cool."

"Sorry for all that crap I said about how you're disrespecting yourself. You know how I get when I'm ranting."

"You know what? You were right. I needed to hear it."

"Happy to be of assistance."

John is incredible. If I were him, I wouldn't be able to even look at me, much less keep being friends with me. But we still feel like Brooke and John, same as always.

Sitting next to one of John's Rubik's Cubes is an origami unicorn. It looks familiar, except that it's painted purple and has sequins for eyes.

"Is that. . . ?" I go over and inspect the unicorn. It was folded from a take-out menu. "Didn't I make this?"

"Yeah."

"I don't remember giving it to you."

"That's because you didn't. I borrowed it."

"You borrowed it?"

"More like stole it. Semantics."

"Why?"

"Are you mad?"

"No, it's OK. You know I make tons of these. But why would you want it?"

"I don't know. It dropped out of your bag and Hailey likes unicorns, so I brought it home for her. She's the one who decorated it, not me."

"I assumed."

"Because I'd use googly eyes instead of sequins."

"It's cute." Hailey glued a satin ribbon on its tail. She also put blue glitter on its horn.

"Oh, it's not only cute. It's purple, it's sparkly, and it's a unicorn. What more do you want?"

I want to ask why the unicorn isn't in Hailey's room, but John's been through enough for one night.

When we go back out to the great room, Hailey's not there. She's shut herself in her room. With the space all to ourselves, I take in how vast it is. John's so lucky to live here. And he's the best kind of lucky – he appreciates what he has.

I look out the big windows. Surrounded by city lights and purple sky, the enormity of being here hits me all over again. It doesn't matter if I can't figure out which way I'm from. All that matters is that I made it to the other side.

This journey wasn't about being with some boy. It was about discovering who I am, realizing what I could be. Moving to New York City was more important than following Scott here. Being with him felt like everything to me. But he was just a catalyst. He was a way of keeping my dream alive. I built him up as someone who would be the answer to everything I wanted.

He's not that boy. No boy is. No one can be everything you want them to be.

The only person I can count on is myself. It's up to me to create the life I want. I can't blame my parents or Scott or anyone else for the way things are.

Now that I know where this life is going, it's time to decide how I'll get there.

TWENTY-FIVE

"Your SAT score from ... let's see ... November was almost perfect. That means colleges will be more lenient about your grades," the college advisor explains.

There was only one college advisor for like 3,000 students at my old school, so after I took the SATs for the first time last May she never called me in or anything. But every senior was required to take the SATs again this fall and now things are different. This advisor is the real deal. She's helping me put together a list of colleges I can actually get into. When I signed up for an appointment with her, I didn't realize how nervous I'd be.

"You have lots of options," she says. "Would you consider going out of state?"

"I don't think so. I really love it here."

"Well, there are plenty of colleges in the city that could work for you. You have a low C average overall, which is close to what most students graduate with. And your recent improvement is a good thing. The only problem is that most of the application deadlines have passed. But you've already applied to a few and we can find some more with later deadlines. There's always community college to fall back on, although I'm sure you'll be accepted somewhere decent. And if you maintain at least a three point eight your first two years, you can transfer to a much better college junior year."

I can't believe this could work out. The colleges I've already applied to are average or below-average ones that take students with lower GPAs like mine. The advisor thinks I have a good chance of getting into any one of them. And there are more colleges I still have time to apply to here in New York, even a few in lower Manhattan where I want to stay.

This is a lot of information. Fortunately, I have a friend who can help me break it down. But before we discuss college, I have to tell her about John.

"I can't believe he likes me," I say. I just told Sadie everything that happened at John's place last night. She wanted to meet at Crumbs, but I insisted on Joe. It's comforting here. I need comforting.

Sadie does not look surprised about John liking me. "I can't believe you didn't know," she says.

"How could you not have told me?"

"How could you not have known?"

"I thought we were just hanging out."

"Oh, please. I could tell from the day you started tutoring. He couldn't wait to talk about you after."

"You should have told me."

"John swore me to secrecy."

"Thanks a lot."

"He has friendship dibs. Anyway, what would you have done? It's not like you'd suddenly start liking someone who wasn't Scott."

Maybe that's what happened with Espresso Boy. Who's here, of course. I was so into telling Sadie everything that happened last night that I didn't even notice him slip in.

"Don't look," I whisper, "but he's here."

"Who, John?"

"No! Espresso Boy."

"This I gotta see," Sadie goes, twisting around.

"I said don't look!"

"Is that him over there? Against the wall?"

"Um-hm."

"Why didn't you tell me he looks like that?"

"Like what?"

"Like cute!"

I *tsk*. "He is not."

"He *so* is. You must still be suffering from Scott-impaired vision."

I steal a peek at Espresso Boy. Naturally, he's picked up on our frenetic vibe and is busy trying to look like he's not watching us watch him. I know Sadie's right about him being cute. But the thought of even thinking some other boy is cute who isn't Scott is making me nauseated.

"He even has a cupcake," Sadie adds. They have

special cupcakes made by one of the celebs who lives nearby. We never know when they'll be here. When they are, Sadie always gets one with her caramel latte. I don't know how she tolerates such extreme sugar overload without bouncing off the walls.

"Lots of people have cupcakes," I say.

"No. Only people who are awesome."

"Do you want me to introduce you?"

"I would if he wasn't smitten with you. I'm doing this thing now where if there's something I want to say, I say it. No more waiting for some mystical right time that never comes and then missing my chance."

"We can find Carlos. We'll just ask the manager."

"That's OK. It's way more fun being consumed by regret."

"I don't get you. Why don't you just ask what his last name is? Or I'm sure they know why he left. Maybe he got transferred to another Rite Aid a few blocks away. He could be right around the corner!"

Sadie sips her latte. "If we were meant to be together, he would have been there when I went in with my note."

"Seriously?"

"Absolutely. Anyway, this is New York! There are plenty of guys."

I still think Sadie should try to find him, but I'm not going to push it. Moving on, I take out my notebook. Sadie said she'd help me figure out my life. She's really good at that kind of thing. It's ironic how I thought she was so annoying at first and now she's like my best friend. I've let April go. Maybe she'll eventually want me back in her life. If she doesn't, there's nothing I can do about it. All I can do is hope that we'll be friends again one day, even though things will never be the same between us.

My phone rings. I'm not surprised at all when the screen tells me that Dad's calling. I let it go to voice mail. He left a bunch of messages last night while I was at John's. He was obviously worried for a change, so I texted him that I was OK and was sleeping over at a friend's. I'm still not ready to talk to him.

I open my notebook to the section with all of my research. There's tons of information I found online about urban planning, running on adrenaline from my night at NYU. And after the college advisor helped me, I had a much better idea of where to find answers.

"So to be an urban planner," I start, "I'll need a master's degree."

"What does your bachelor's have to be in?"

"It can be in a few different areas, but I like environmental studies the best. Then I can focus on how green building design helps improve people's emotional and physical health."

Sadie lurches off her chair, checking for something outside.

"What's wrong?"

"Nothing." She sits back down. "I was just checking to make sure the rest of reality was still out there."

"Why, because I'm talking about college? So is everyone else."

"No, everyone else was talking about college when apps were due. Remember? Back when you haphazardly applied to random colleges just because they're here?"

"Well excuse me for not wanting to leave New York. It took me for ever to get here. Leaving would be stupid."

"I'm not saying you should leave. There has to be a programme here that fits what you want. Have you researched which colleges have rolling admissions? Or later deadlines?"

Flipping the page triumphantly, I pass the notebook over to Sadie. "Done and done." I wish I had better choices, but the important thing is that I start using education as a way to get where I want to go.

She takes a look at my list. "Nice. You have to hurry, though."

"I know, I'm sending in my apps this week. And they all have majors that work, so. . ."

Sadie beams at me. "How proud am I?"

"Stop."

"No, I'm serious. This is . . . John always says how you could be doing so much more with your life, and I have to agree. It's like you finally get it."

Espresso Boy is sneaking looks at me. I take a flyer for guitar lessons that someone left on the table and start folding a butterfly.

"I don't think you need my help," Sadie says. "It looks like you already have everything planned out."

"No, I need you for something."

"What?"

"To tell me I can do this. Am I too late?"

"Absolutely not. It's never too late to turn your life around."

I really hope she's right.

Before Sadie leaves, I slide a note into her bag. I wrote her a warm fuzzy after I woke up at John's this morning, overcome by a sense of urgency. I need the people who support me to know how much they mean to me. I wish Sadie didn't have to go, but she has to get ready for this meet-and-greet thing tonight. One of the colleges she applied to is having an open house. Their philosophy seems to be that if they offer up snacks, people will be more likely to go there if they get in.

Sadie's always so busy. If she's not killing herself over school, she's tutoring or doing random-acts-of-kindness outreach or reading to kids at the hospital or a zillion other things. I don't know how she does it all. Just thinking about her packed schedule makes me exhausted. At the same time, it makes me want to do more. There are so many possibilities waiting to be discovered. Any of them could shape my future.

After my origami butterfly is done, I prop it up against the windowsill. I love finding creative energy in unexpected places. Like these little stick figures that are painted on some street corners in my neighbourhood. I've seen a few of them in different colours. Even though I have no idea what they represent, to someone else they mean something and that's awesome. I wonder what the next person who sits here will think of my butterfly. Will they even notice it's there? Will they pick it up, wonder who made it and why it was left behind? If the right person finds it, it might count as a random act of kindness.

When I leave, Espresso Boy doesn't even look up from his book. It's not until I'm halfway down the block that he comes running after me.

"Wait up," he says. "I'm . . . I was in Joe."

"I know."

We stop walking. Then we're just standing there, looking at each other.

"Did you get my note?" he asks.

"Yeah. It was really nice of you. Sorry I didn't call."

"Why didn't you?"

"Honestly?"

"Go for it."

"I was interested in someone else. And I knew you wouldn't want to hear that."

He nods slowly, looking miserable. "It would have been nice to at least know what was going on with you. It took me for ever to write that note, which I know sounds crazy since it was so short, but it took me a long time to get those few words right."

I try to think of what I should say. But I don't really know what that is.

"Even after I wrote it, I wasn't sure I'd have the

courage to give it to you. Every day you didn't call was like this growing disappointment. I had to know if there was a chance for me, which is why you now have a crazy guy following you down the street."

How wild is this? I was so wrapped up in my own drama that I was completely oblivious someone else was having drama about me. I never thought I could be a major issue in someone else's life that way. Which is strange because look at the whole Scott thing. He was completely oblivious to how much he meant to me. It's unbelievable how you can affect someone else so deeply and never know.

I had no idea how much courage it took Espresso Boy to give me that note.

"You must think I'm deranged," he says.

"No I don't. It's just that I can't get into another relationship right now. My boyfriend and I broke up three days ago."

"Oh. Sorry. I shouldn't have bothered you. Timing is everything, huh?"

When Espresso Boy goes back inside, I watch him sitting down at his table through the window. And that's when I realize that I don't know his name. He wrote it on his note, but I forget what it is. I didn't even ask.

I make a resolution to never let something like this happen again. Even if I'm not interested in someone who likes me, the least I can do is ask what their name is. I want deeper connections with the people around me. I need to reach out more. Because not everyone leaves. Sometimes if you reach out, the person you're trying to reach will be right there waiting.

Regret is a nasty thing. I hate that I wasted all those years rebelling against a system I could have used to my advantage. If my grades were what they should have been, I wouldn't be worrying over colleges right now. I'd be able to kick back and enjoy the ride. Instead, I'm scared that I might not get in anywhere. I know what the college advisor said about my SAT score, but I doubt they're going to care that my grades improved last marking period or that I'm a peer tutor. Acceptance committees look at all four years of high school, especially junior year. Of course that's when I was the angriest. I can't believe I was so stupid. All of my rebellion did absolutely nothing for me or anyone else. I hardly remember how I thought I could change things. Having a tangible goal I feel passionate about makes all the difference.

So, yeah. It's time for an overhaul of priorities. Working towards my future career. Using my talents to help people. Creating a life that means something. The Knowing tells me that these things are possible.

I take out my wish box. Sifting through the notes I've written, I can't believe how many of them have to do with Scott. What about what I wanted, just for me? Didn't I want anything unrelated to some boy?

Apparently not. I take out every single note I've

ever written about Scott. Then I rip each one into tiny pieces.

Tonight is all about making new wishes. On my way home, I went to Kate's Paperie and got this gorgeous stationery. It's a pack of handmade papers in all different patterns. Each paper has something unique about it, like cool patterns or pressed flowers or frayed edges. It's exactly the kind of special paper I want to use for my renovated wish box.

I also bought a pack of Gelly Roll Lightning pens. I uncap the green one and start writing about my future. I write about how I want next year to be. I write about how I want the rest of this year to be, starting now. About the kind of boy I want to be with. Although I don't think I'll want to be with anyone for a really long time. Being with a boy isn't the most important thing, anyway. The most important thing is that I'm figuring out who I am. When I can accept who I am instead of fighting it, then I'll be ready for a real relationship.

After I carefully arrange all of the new notes in my wish box, I examine the box itself. Decorating the outside of your wish box is crucial. Most of the images I taped on are of Scott and New York. I keep the New York ones on, peeling off the pictures of Scott. I rip those up and throw them away. Then I go online to look for images of green spaces, the High Line, city lights, skylines, rooftops, water towers . . . all of the things that speak to me. My heart keeps hurting as I do all this, but the distraction makes it hurt a little less.

When the phone rings, I check the time. I'm shocked that I've been working on my wish box for over three hours.

"Hello?"

"I found him," Sadie says.

"Who?"

"Who do you think? Carlos!"

"Where?"

"You know that meet-and-greet I went to?"

"Yeah."

"He was there."

"Dude!"

"I know. Too bad I was a complete dumbass about it."

"Doubtful. He's probably in love with you already."

"Not after what I did. I saw him standing by the refreshment table and . . . OK, at first I couldn't believe it was really him. So I went up to him and I was like, 'Carlos?' And he goes, 'How do I know you?' So I said that I sometimes go into Rite Aid and he was like, 'I knew I knew you.' Then I asked — I could *not* be more mortified — I asked if he was working at the meet-and-greet. I thought he was with the caterer or something."

"Oooh."

"He was like, 'Uh, no. I applied here.' Can you believe it? We might actually be going to the same college! Not like it matters. Could I have *been* more insulting?"

"You didn't know. I'm sure it was nothing."

"Oh, it was something. I spent the whole time

apologizing for my dumbass ways. I was such a freak about it that he didn't even ask for my number."

"Blerg."

"Good thing I asked for his. And he gave it to me!"

"Sweet! See, I told you he didn't care. When are you calling him?"

"How long should I wait?"

"No games. You should call him when you want to call him."

"Oh, so, like, every second?"

"Where's your boy confidence?"

"Just because I whipped up a speck of boy confidence to ask for his number doesn't mean it came with the manual. These things are tricky. If I call him right away, that might be a turnoff. But if I wait too long, he could be going out with someone else. So what's the perfect amount of waiting time?"

"You're asking the wrong person." Clearly, I know nothing about boys. I'm the last person anyone should be asking for boy advice.

But life advice? For the first time ever, I think I might have some to offer.

TWENTY-SIX

Sunday nights always come with a sinking feeling of impending doom. That's why Mondays intrinsically suck. Everyone's drained and cranky, just waiting for it to be Friday again. As if Mondays weren't bad enough, of course we're working in pairs today in the Box. It's a shame that what used to be the best class is now the worst. All it took was one person to ruin everything. Because of Scott, every part of school sucks worse than it did before. Which makes it really hard to keep up my new academically motivated attitude.

It's absurd how I would have given anything to be with Scott before and now I hate that I'm stuck with him. Meanwhile, Scott seems fine.

Underneath all of the effort I'm making to turn my life around, I'm a mess. It's only been six days since we broke up. I've tried to fill the void with new priorities, new plans, new goals. And I'm actually excited about my future. But my heart still hurts. It's like this constant ache that dulls everything else. I can't imagine feeling normal again.

"So. . ." Scott looks over the project sheet we're supposed to be working on. "What do you think?"

Here's what I think:

I think moving here for you was the right thing to do.

I think you broke up with me because you're afraid of having something real.

I think this blows.

"I think you're going back to Leslie," I say.

I don't know where that came from. I've been worrying that part of the reason Scott broke up with me is so he could get back together with Leslie. It would make sense. Leslie is fun. I'm serious. Leslie is simple. I come with baggage. Leslie isn't as stressed about where things are going. She's just happy to be going anywhere at all.

"Uh, no," Scott says. "I'm not."

"You're not?"

"Why would you think that?"

"I don't know. Because you were saying how you wanted to keep things casual. She seems . . . uncomplicated."

"She is. That's why I'm not interested."

"I thought you wanted uncomplicated."

"I wanted you."

"Then why. . . ?"

"You're the one who didn't want me."

"Of course I wanted you!"

The kids sitting next to us suddenly stop talking. I pretend to concentrate on my project sheet. After they start talking again, I go, "Why are you twisting everything around?"

"You're the one who was unhappy with the way things were. You wanted this serious commitment and everything."

"You don't think Leslie wants that? All girls want that."

"Do you have any idea how threatened Leslie is by you?"

"Hilarious."

"She is. She could tell I liked you more than I admitted. Or even realized. It's like she knew what was going to happen with us way before I did."

"Oh."

"That's why she'd always bring you up in conversations, like she was trying to test my response to hearing your name or something."

"How do you know all this?"

"She wrote me the world's longest email right after I got together with you. I don't know why she sent it. She knew I chose you."

"She was trying to get you back."

"Well, it was too late."

Is Scott trying to say that it's also too late for us? Because he's making it sound like the breakup was more my fault than his. Which is ridiculous. Only . . . would I even want to get back together with him? A week ago, I would have said absolutely. Now I'm not so sure.

I've been looking back on everything and I don't think I liked the person I was with Scott. I mean, being his girlfriend was amazing. But I was insecure around him. I'd never been insecure around boys before. Every time the phone rang, there was this jolt of adrenaline at the possibility that it was Scott, but there was also a twinge of fear. Like maybe it was Scott, but he was calling to say that we didn't belong together. I never felt like he was completely mine. I couldn't count on him the way I can count on John.

John fights for me no matter what. He keeps trying to break down my wall. He never gives up on who I am or who I could be. He doesn't run away when things get complicated. Even when John was mad at me, he didn't let that stop him from caring about me.

Here's the thing. I could spend the rest of my life chasing that amazing feeling I had every time I even thought about Scott. Physical attraction that strong is addictive. And knowing that kind of magic isn't just a fantasy makes me want to find it again. But what about being with someone who makes me a better person? What about sharing my life with someone who adores me as much as I adore him, whom I can always count on, who helps me find my way when I'm lost?

If I could find both intense physical attraction and strong emotional support with one boy, that would be perfect. But if it has to be one or the other? The choice is clear.

*

Whenever my mom calls, I usually try to keep the conversation short. I figure the less time she has to insult me, the better.

This time is different.

I've just told her all about meeting with the college advisor and visiting NYU and how I want to be an urban planner.

"That's wonderful," Mom says. "It sounds like you have a lot going on."

"I do."

"I'm relieved that you're figuring things out."

"Yeah. Maybe I'm not a loser after all."

"Who ever said you were a loser?"

"You did. I mean, you implied it. All those times you said I wasn't working hard enough. It felt like you gave up on me."

"I said those things because I wanted more for you, Brooke."

She sounds hurt. Now I feel bad.

"No, you were right. I wasn't working hard enough. And that's changed now. But why do you have to be so critical all the time? Why can't you be supportive? You say you're trying to help me, but all it does is make me feel worse."

Mom doesn't say anything for a long time.

"Mom?"

"I'm sorry I've been so hard on you," she says, her voice cracking on the *you*. "I just want you to be successful."

"You can stop worrying. Things are working out now."

Uncomfortable silence.

"So," she says, "do you think you'll be home for winter break?"

"I'm not sure."

"What about spring break?"

"I might be staying here for both. I really need to figure everything out."

"Oh. Well, if you don't come home I'll see you at graduation. It would be nice to see you sometime in the next five months, though."

I get that this is hard for her. But going back for Christmas break was excruciating. It felt like I was taking a step backwards when all I wanted to do was keep moving forward. New York is my home now. The Knowing tells me that I'll be going to college here. I won't have to leave unless I want to, and I can't imagine ever wanting to.

"You could always come visit," I suggest.

"It's been a big year for you. I wish I hadn't missed it."

"You didn't, Mom. I told you everything." Everything except for what happened with Scott. I wasn't going to tell her anything about him, but I had to because Dad knew. There was the possibility that Dad would tell Mom. So I told her Scott was this boy I met here. Scott agreed to tell my dad the same thing if it ever came up. Luckily, Dad just assumed he was from here.

"Are you still getting along with your father?"

"Mostly. But I really miss your cooking."

Mom laughs. "I never thought I'd hear you say that."

"Oh, I'm saying it."

"Even my meat loaf?"

"Especially your meat loaf."

More uncomfortable silence.

"Well," I say, "I better go."

"Call if you need me."

I can tell she's sad about being apart. But in a way, the distance is helping both of us. Sometimes you just need room to appreciate what you have.

TWENTY-SEVEN

I thought tutoring John would be awkward from now on. But it feels the same as always. At least it does to me.

John isn't mad at me any more. The night I slept over, he felt really bad for me. My dad and I haven't said more than three words to each other since our fight, and that was a week ago.

There's this SAT prep course John's taking. He already took the course last year, but his mom wants him to take the SATs again to try for a higher score. I'm supposed to help him with practice exams until he takes it again in March. We've been working on this one essay in the writing section for ever. It wants to know if memories help or hinder your success.

"What's that shape that's like..." John tries to remember. "The one with sides that are all—a rhomboid."

"Like a parallelogram?"

"Except the sides aren't parallel."

"You mean a rhombus?"

"No, that thing with—"

"A trapezoid?"

"Yes!" John pounds the table. "That one!"

"Can you guys keep it down over there?" Sadie jokes from the next table. "Some of us are trying to learn."

"Rhomboid," John informs her. He gives her a thumbs-up. Then he writes down whatever it is he was trying to say about memories.

While he's finishing the essay, I go up to Mr Peterson to ask a question. Except it's not a real question. It's just an excuse to sneak something into his bag. When he turns away to get a book off the shelf, I drop a copy of my report card into his open messenger bag. There's a warm-fuzzy Post-it note stuck on saying thanks for pushing me to be better. Out of all the teachers and other school types who have pressured me to improve over the years, Mr Peterson is the only one who gave me a good enough reason to do it.

After tutoring, I walk out with John and Sadie as usual. But instead of Sadie and I walking home together, John waits until she leaves. Then he says, "Can I come over?"

"What for?"

"Jeez, I didn't know I needed an engraved invitation."

"No, you totally can. It's just that you've never come over before."

"Exactly. You've been to my place twice already. Don't you think I should catch up?"

So John comes over. As usual, Dad's still at work.

"It's so quiet here," John says. "Is it always this quiet?"

"Pretty much. My dad works late."

"That rules. I never get the place to myself. Even

when it's just me and my mom and Hailey, it feels like eight people are there. Must be an estrogen thing. Having girls around always seems like more people than it is. OK, what am I talking about? That SAT prep fried my brain."

We go to my room. I wish I'd known John would be coming over. It's a disaster in here.

"You have the *Office Space* stapler!" John shouts.

"I do?"

He goes over to my desk and picks it up. "I didn't know you had this!"

"Neither did I. I just thought it was a stapler."

"This isn't any old stapler. It's a Rio Red Collector's Edition Swingline. Remember that poster I have with the smoking red stapler?"

"Oh, yeah. I like that one."

"Where did you get this?"

"My dad's interior designer picked it out."

John's all obsessing over the stapler.

"Why don't you just get one?" I say.

"Oh, I will. It never even occurred to me to just, like, get one. This is so cool!"

I turn on some music. John sprawls on my bed and I take the beanbag.

"Listen," he says. "You know that thing I said to you the night you slept over?"

"You mean about—"

"Yeah, that. Just forget about that. Erase it from your big brain."

"Sadie's the only one allowed to say my brain is big."

"No, she gave me privileges. Anyway. I want you to pretend you never heard it."

"Heard what?"

"Do you not know what I'm talking about?"

"Yeah, I meant . . . forget it."

"Oh! Like – OK. See, I told you my brain is fried. My communication skills are even more horrocious than usual."

"Horrocious?"

"It's a combination of horrific and atrocious." John looks at my collection of city skyline prints on the wall. "I should probably get up and check out your stuff. This being my first time in your room and all. Tragically, I am too lazy to do so."

"That's OK. I'm feeling pretty exhausted myself."

"How are you holding up?"

"You mean . . . with the whole breakup thing?"

"Yeah."

"Not great. I'm distracting myself with college plans."

"Sadie told me. It's awesome that you're taking your life more seriously."

John makes me smile. He says these things that, coming from anyone else, would sound ridiculous. But with John, it's really the way he feels.

"You've helped me a lot," I tell him.

"How?"

"You helped me figure out that I want to be an urban planner. All those times on the High Line and walking around with you were like... It made me realize that if the two of us feel the way we do about New York, lots of other people must feel the same way. And that I can actually dedicate my life to improving how people connect with the city."

John twists around on my bed so his chin is resting on the edge of my mattress and his legs are dangling off the other side. "I helped?" he says.

"Totally. You were helping me the whole time just by being you. I really appreciate everything you've done."

"Wow. I didn't even know I was doing anything."

"Well, you were."

"That's intense."

He's right. It is intense.

John's staring at me. I stare back. It's like we get each other without having to say anything.

"Can I ask you something?" he says. "As my tutor?"

"Anything."

"Do you think college will be an epic fail for me?"

"Of course not."

"You can be honest."

"I *am* being honest. You're going to love it. That college that doesn't give grades sounds perfect for you. Aren't they all about creativity and diversity there?"

"Yeah, but what if I don't get in?"

"What if you do?"

"What if I do and I'm not good enough?"

I had no idea John was worried about college. He always seems so certain. I've been a little concerned about how he'll adjust academically, but I'm not worried about him socially at all. If anyone's going to take advantage of everything college life has to offer, it's John.

"You're better than good enough," I say. "You're outstanding."

"I'm sorry, have you seen my transcript?"

"Who cares? No grade could ever quantify how smart you are."

"Too bad colleges don't think like that."

"If they don't take you, it's their loss."

"You really believe that?"

"Totally." It's so weird how this whole time I thought John had some secret to success that he wasn't sharing with anyone. He's never let his guard down before, which I didn't even know he had. I thought I was the only one with armour. It's surprising that he has hidden insecurities and doubts, too, but it's also comforting. It makes me feel less alone.

When I hear the front door open, I can't believe John's been here long enough for Dad to get home. We've just been talking this whole time, but it doesn't feel like he's even been here for an hour. The clock says he's been here for almost three.

Dad must have seen John's coat and bag near the door because he comes right back to my room. He never does that. He usually comes home, puts some takeout on the kitchen counter, and heads for his laptop in the living room. But here he is. Dad. Hovering in my doorway. Staring at John sprawled on my bed.

"Hey, Mr Greene!" John jumps up and goes over to my dad. "Awesome to finally meet you, sir. I'm John Dalton. Of the High Line Daltons." John extends his hand for Dad to shake. "Sorry. Joke. Horrocious brain fry."

Dad stares at John. They shake hands.

"You should really know that Brooke is the best tutor I've ever had. Seriously, the girl has changed my life. I'd be a mess without her."

"Stop," I say. He's so embarrassing.

Then we're all just standing around, waiting for someone else to say something.

Eventually, Dad says, "Brooke, I need to talk to you."

That chips away a piece of John's confidence. "Oh, should I – I can go. Yeah, I'll go." I follow John to the front door. As he's putting on his coat he whispers, "Call me if you need anything."

"I will."

"You can always stay at my place again. You know that, right?"

"I do."

Back in my room, Dad's sitting at my desk. I straighten the duvet, then sit on my bed. I don't know why I'm so nervous.

"It's occurred to me that you require more structure," he says.

"Meaning?"

"Meaning you can't just run around like this. I was

trying to give you some space. I know what it's like living with your mother and I wanted you to have more freedom here. But you're staying out late . . . I didn't even know where you went that night you didn't come home—"

"I didn't think you'd care."

"Of course I cared. That's why I kept calling you. You wouldn't be here if I didn't care. I thought that with you living here, I'd be in your life more."

"Things can't just suddenly change because you want them to, Dad. You have to make them change."

"I know. That's what I'm doing." Dad takes one of my Gelly Roll pens out of their glass jar. He taps it against my calculus book. "No boys in your room. I was that age once. I know how they think. They shouldn't be in here."

"Fine."

"No staying out all night. You have to get permission if you want to sleep over at a friend's house. And I don't want you out so late on school nights. You need to be home by . . . let's say nine thirty. No, nine."

"OK."

Dad looks as sad as Mom sounded on the phone last time I talked to her.

"Sorry I'm not around more," he says. "My plan was to get home earlier and have dinner with you every night. I know it's not fair for you to be here alone. But I don't know if things will change. They probably won't. Are you OK with that?"

"I'll have to be."

Dad sighs. "Guess I kind of suck at this, huh?"

"You're not that bad. I mean . . . there's always room for improvement."

He laughs. "You're right about that."

After the night I stormed out, I was so afraid Dad would send me back to New Jersey. That week he didn't talk to me was the worst. But it sounds like he was afraid, too. Afraid of what he might hear if he asked for the truth. Maybe even afraid that I didn't want to live with him any more. Because if everything he's told me is true, then he really does want me here. He's just not ready to overhaul his life for me the way I did for Scott. Plus, he did the whole rule thing backwards. It's not the best that he's so clueless, but it's not the worst, either.

"By the way," Dad says, "if you stay in New York for college, your room will always be here. You're welcome anytime."

"You mean you're not turning it back into an office?"

"I have enough office at the office. Anyway, you know I prefer working in the living room."

"True. Um . . . can we maybe go running on Sundays? Like we were supposed to?"

"Absolutely. Should we wait until it gets warmer?"

"Sure." I don't know if we'll ever go running every week. But it's OK. Whatever happens, I know that right in this moment, Dad means it and he's trying.

"Have you eaten yet?" he says.

"No, I'm starving."

"How do you feel about pizza?"

"Extra cheese and garlic?"

"Sounds like a plan. I'll make the call."

It's cool that we're eating dinner together for once, but I'm not deluded. I know that tomorrow things will probably go back to the way they've been. It's too soon for any big changes to happen, if they're ever going to happen at all. But the possibility of change makes me happy. It gives me hope again.

TWENTY-EIGHT

The Zen garden was so desolate all winter. I only came out here a few times, wrapped up in my puffy coat, watching the city lights sparkle in the cold night. I haven't seen Ree in a while. I wonder how she's doing, if she still comes out here to sketch the moon.

I love being back in the garden now that it's warmer. I can't wait for the sunflowers to grow again. And I'm excited about this walk we're about to go on. I'm just waiting for everyone to get here.

Looking around for John, I find him crossing the street. I can tell it's him even from this far away. I like being able to watch him when he doesn't know I'm watching. Whenever we have plans to do something, I always get this happy feeling of anticipation. I love spending time with John. He's the first person I've ever felt totally comfortable with. I don't have to think about how to act when I'm with him. It's such a relief to just relax and be myself, especially since I'm starting to understand who that is. He makes me feel like nothing I could do would make him like me any less. And that's an amazing feeling.

When John finds me he says, "Wanna go for a walk?"

"Like I'd miss our vernal equinox walk."

"And vernal equinox resolution. It's kind of like an autumnal equinox resolution, only better."

"Do you know what your resolution is?"

"You know what it is." He looks at me with intense eyes.

I feel my cheeks get hot. It didn't used to bother me when John said stuff like that back when I found out he liked me. But now it affects me. Not to the point where I'd want to stop being friends or anything. We're better friends than ever. It's just . . . the way he looks at me. It's intense, is all.

Sadie has a theory that when I was infatuated with Scott, I wasn't able to accurately process any other boy's behavior. It was like I was perceiving all the other boys through some kind of filter. Now that filter is off and everything is much clearer.

"Happy spring!" Sadie yells from the walking path. We get up from our rock and make our way down to her, stepping on the other big rocks as we go.

"Can you believe this weather?" I say.

"I know," she says. "It's like spring knew we were going to celebrate it."

"Spring totally knew," Carlos says. The way he agrees with Sadie is so cute. He's completely smitten.

I could not have been prouder of Sadie when she called Carlos. She lost almost all of her boy confidence after he gave her his number. She was convinced that he thought she was a complete freak and only gave her his number to be nice, so after obsessing for days over whether to call him she wasn't even going to call. But then Sadie remembered how she promised herself she wouldn't have any more regrets.

It's obvious that Carlos was stoked by her decision.

As we start walking downtown in the twilight, more city lights blink on. This is the best time for a walk, with everything the night can bring just waiting to be discovered.

I take a piece of paper folded into a trapezoid out of my bag. I slip it into John's back pocket.

"What's that?" he says.

"Just something."

"What is it?"

"A note. A warm fuzzy, more specifically."

"You are so in love with those!" Sadie raves. She gazes adoringly at Carlos. "I transformed Brooke from an aloof, cynical person into someone who writes warm fuzzies."

"Hey," John says. "You can't take all the credit. Let the record show that other people were involved in that transformation."

"Sorry, John. You rule as well."

"You guys make me sound like an extra-credit project," I say. "Don't listen to them, Carlos. I wasn't aloof."

Carlos smiles knowingly. He's only been with Sadie for two months, but that's more than enough time to understand how giving she is.

"Is it the warm fuzzy you promised me?" John asks.

"That would be the one. You should read it later." We're passing an enormous building with huge loft spaces. The lights are on in the penthouse, which has a spectacular glass wall. I tilt my head way back and look up. You can totally see in. It would be so cool to have a home like that one day.

I look up a lot more these days. To me, it feels like hope. Now I know that the chances for happiness are infinite. Anything can happen. And there are people who will stick by me even though I'll always be a work in progress.

John is staring at me. I can feel his stare against the side of my face.

"What?" I go.

"I love watching you when you see something you like."

"You have to quit saying things like that."

"Why?"

"Because I know you like me."

"So? Does that mean I can't be honest any more?"

"This isn't awkward at all," Sadie tells Carlos.

"Sorry, guys. I keep explaining to John that friends don't say things like that to their friends."

"No, but a friend who's in love with a friend does."

Pause. Did John just tell me he loves me?

Sadie and John exchange a look. No one knows how I'm going to react. Including me.

"It's OK if you don't feel the same way," John says. "I get it. I just wanted you to know."

One of the most amazing things that can happen is finding someone who sees everything you are and won't let you be anything less. They see the potential of you. They see endless possibilities. And through their eyes, you start to see yourself the same way. As someone who matters. As someone who can make a difference in this world.

If you're lucky enough to find that person, never let them go.

I grab his hand. This time, I won't let go.

ACKNOWLEDGMENTS

Warm fuzzies with extra sparkle go out to:

Kendra Levin & Regina Hayes
In the world of editing, you are gifted with The Knowing.

My Penguin family
The ones who make it all happen.

Jim Hoover & Marc Tauss
For turning my dream cover into reality.

David Letterman
Who sparked my passion for New York City.

Gillian MacKenzie & Kirsten Wolf
For always having my back.

Laurie Halse Anderson, Sarah Dessen, and Meg Cabot
From whom I've learned so much.

Dr Pat Sharkey, NYU Department of Sociology
For enlightening me about neighbourhood effects.

Paul Simon
Back in the day, you were the soundtrack of my future.

Jim Downs
Fellow lover of the Energy, fellow winner of the race.

Joe Torello
Who knows all about chasing the dream.

Pierre
Who understands about the High Line.

And especially my readers
Your excitement and support help me to always dream big.
Infinite thanks to you.